Despite being a full-time chef, Adam Longden fulfilled a lifelong ambition when his debut fiction novel *The Caterpillar Girl* was published in October 2016. This was followed by its sequel, *Seaside Skeletons,* the third book in the series *Asylum,* and a separate novella, *Eva: A Grown-up Fairy Tale.*

Adam has three children and resides in the East Midlands where the majority of his books are set.

This book is dedicated to my children: Max, Madeleine and Emily.

Adam Longden

THE MEDDLING GHOSTS

AUSTIN MACAULEY PUBLISHERS™

LONDON • CAMBRIDGE • NEW YORK • SHARJAH

A CIP catalogue record for this title is available from the British Library.

ISBN 9781398465008 (Paperback)
ISBN 9781398465015 (ePub e-book)

www.austinmacauley.com

First Published 2022
Austin Macauley Publishers Ltd
1 Canada Square
Canary Wharf
London
E14 5AA

The Cast of Ghosts

PAUL BEARER—Former funeral director, died from a broken heart.

COLONEL PINE—Former military man, died during 'coitus' with a much younger woman.

PASTOR CARBONARA—Former Italian-American priest, drank himself to death.

A. CORDINGLEY—Former IT consultant, choked on a fishbone.

PENNY DREADFUL—Former schoolmistress, died of pneumonia.

SAM HANDWICH—Former stable boy, kicked in the head by a horse.

CALYPSO—Former brothel girl, died from a laudanum overdose.

JUNIPER—A twin. Former folk healer, accused of witchcraft, died from hanging.

ABSINTHE—A twin. Sister of Juniper, died from hanging.

LEOFWINE—Juniper's black cat, drowned in a well.

Chapter One

The heavy front door of Cuckoo House slammed shut, disturbing Elaine Berridge, asleep on the sofa, indulging in her daily post-work snooze.

A teenage girl, her curly hair and burgundy school jumper soaked through, burst into the lounge. She threw the guitar case and rucksack she was carrying onto the floor. The guitar emitted an indignant, resonant twang from within that lingered.

Elaine studied her daughter, Leah—13 going on 30—through half-closed eyes and the grey veil of depression, as the real world swam back into focus. The girl's face was a furious pink, her glare accusatory. Leah pulled a stray, wet curl from her mouth and said, "Asleep as usual. I bloody well knew it!"

A gaggle of the resident ghosts, mainly the younger, more inquisitive ones, gathered on the landing above—Sam Handwich and the twins, Absinthe and Juniper, trailed by Leofwine, the cat. The cat rubbed himself against Sam's baggy, long socks, nestled around his ankles. Sam knelt down on bare, scabbed knees to pet him. Penny Dreadful, the mother hen of the brood, joined them to listen to the row that had broken out downstairs.

"Why does she let her speak to her like that?" said Juniper.

"It wouldn't have happened in my day," said Penny. "She would have got a good thrashing. The girl's a brat—I blame those gadgets."

"But what's got her goat this time?" said Juniper.

"They've forgotten to pick her up from her guitar lesson," said Sam.

"The boy may be dim-witted, but in this instance, he's right," a voice from behind said. "Today is Tuesday. Leah has a guitar lesson every Tuesday after school, term time only, 3:30 till 4:30 p.m." It was Cordingley, Andrew Cordingley, but everyone called him by his last name: a bit of a know-it-all, a nosey parker. Being the most recently deceased of the group by some distance—centuries, in fact—he didn't quite fit in. He still hadn't got used to his recent, otherworldly predicament, and they hadn't got used to him—or the chip on his shoulder.

"Sshh! I'm trying to listen," said Absinthe. Sam stuck his face through the bannister rails as if to hear better.

"I've just walked miles in the pouring rain with a guitar case!" Leah shouted.

"Why? What day is it?"

"Tuesday. Guitar lesson, remember?"

"Well, why didn't you phone me?" Elaine sat up on the sofa, feeling around for her phone. The blanket she had been lying under slipped off her shoulders to reveal the nurse's uniform she was still wearing from work.

"I did. And texted—several times."

Elaine located her phone. The screen confirmed what Leah was saying. "Oh, sorry, darling. It was on silent. I just wanted 40 winks."

"You always want 40 winks! That's all you do—sleep, or row with Dad."

"Look, I'm not getting into that now. I've just woken up: I've got a headache—"

"There's a surprise."

Elaine gave her daughter a look. "Leah, I said I was sorry. Why didn't you phone Jake, anyway? He could have woken me. Actually, is he here? I didn't hear him come back." She looked confused for a second.

"I don't know. I've just got here, haven't I? And I did text him. He's probably in his pit with his headphones on, playing his stupid games, talking to his stupid mates."

"All right. It's not your brother's fault. Besides, you're home now, that's the main thing. No harm done."

"No, except I've probably got pneumonia." Upstairs, Penny rolled her eyes.

"I doubt that, it's only a bit of rain. I'd get those wet things off, though. Do you want a cup of tea?" Elaine said.

"No. I'm going to get changed." Leah pulled her phone from a pocket on her rucksack, scrutinised it, then left the room.

Elaine shivered and wrapped the blanket back around her. Despite it being springtime, Cuckoo House—formerly The Cuckoo Inn—hadn't warmed up yet due to the thick, stone walls. By the end of summer, when it did just about warm up, autumn arrived and the house turned cold again—a perpetual source of irritation. She groaned as the prospect of making dinner hit her: the drudgery of it, the routine; she barely had the will to get up off the sofa, never mind rustle up a meal for four.

Leah headed upstairs, holding her phone in front of her as if it was a water diviner, eyes glued to the screen, thumbs busy. The ghosts pressed themselves against the walls and bannister as she approached. It wasn't pleasant for either party when a human walked straight through a ghost. Cordingley looked disdainful as she passed. He pushed his glasses up onto his nose. Sam had a dreamy look on his face. Absinthe blew on Leah's hair, mischievous as ever. Leah shuddered, feeling a sudden chill. *Pneumonia, I bloody knew it*, she thought, intending to announce the fact very shortly on Snapchat.

Sam went to follow Leah, but she pulled up abruptly outside her room. He froze. She held her phone aloft, tousled her hair, and adopted her ubiquitous duck-face pout to take a selfie of her bedraggled state. Penny dragged Sam away just as the phone flashed and clicked. On inspection, Leah didn't like the image that greeted her; she looked too pale and spotty, and her hair had gone all curly. In the corner of the screen was a little chink of white: Sam's blurred hand. Leah rubbed at the screen, but the mark remained. *Funny*, she thought, deleting the picture, before entering her room.

Unperturbed, Sam made to follow her again. Penny kept a firm grasp on his collar and gave him a look that said, 'Oh no, you don't!' The bedroom door closed. "Idiot boy!" she hissed. "You nearly got caught!" Sam looked shameful.

"He's getting to that age. He's in love. Wants to go in there and watch her get undressed," mocked Absinthe.

"Getting to that age! What a preposterous thing to say. He's been 'that age' for centuries—you mean *she's* getting to that age," said Cordingley.

More footsteps were heard on the stairs. It was Elaine. She was heading to the boy's room at the other end of the galleried landing. The ghosts tiptoed to the corner to watch. Elaine knocked on her son's door. "Jake, are you home?" She couldn't hear the misogynistic cacophony of rap music pounding away that he was partial to: 'bitches' this, 'hoes' that. But then again, he was usually thoughtful enough not to have it blaring out when she was trying to sleep. *He was a good boy*, she reflected, opening the door. "Oh, you are here," she said.

Jake was hunched in front of his TV screen, standard-issue controller in hand, headset covering his ears, baseball cap on backwards. "Back in a minute," he said into the mouthpiece, removing the headset. "Hi." He swivelled around in his chair to face her.

"I wish you'd sit up straight when you're playing on that thing. You'll end up with a hunched back." Jake offered a sheepish smile in response. "Anyway, how was your day? I didn't hear you come back."

"No, you were asleep, so I left you to it."

"Oh, thanks. By the way, did Leah text you earlier?"

"I don't know. Why?" He reached for his phone. There was a text and a missed call from his sister: *'Wake Mum up. I need picking up from school!'* "Er, yes, looks like it," he said. "Sorry."

"Never mind, she's back now. She's not too happy, though."

"That makes a change." Jake fiddled with the mouthpiece of his headset, keen to get back to it. "Er, what's for dinner?"

"Don't know. Something from the freezer, I expect. Have you got any homework?"

"Not sure, a bit I think."

"Best get it out of the way then." Elaine gave the peak of his cap a tug, then left the room, closing the door behind her. She heard a deep, throaty chuckle from Jake as he returned to his friends. It still freaked her out, how his voice had changed so drastically—like a man trapped in a boy's body and clothes.

Back downstairs, Elaine opened the fridge, stared lifelessly into it, sighed, then closed it again. She crouched to open the freezer door and was met with frosted drawers, caked with ice. The sight of them overwhelmed her, and she wanted to cry. Instead, she went to pull one of them out, but the drawer put up a fight. She swore and yanked it open. Half-empty boxes and bags of what she called 'frozen crap' were extracted and carried through to the kitchen.

Dinner took all of two minutes to put on. Potato waffles on a tray, breaded chicken on a tray, frozen peas clattered into a pan. After rinsing her hands, she made her way back to the lounge to put the news on. She had no intention of watching it; it was purely for company. On the way, she passed the Everest-sized ironing pile, one of her greatest adversaries. It mocked her, again, overwhelmed her. She wished, just for one day, she could step out of her life—be someone else, be somewhere else.

TV turned on, Elaine returned to the sofa and opened up Facebook on her phone. Out in the hallway, the stairs creaked and she looked up, expecting one of the children to come in. They didn't. She went back to her phone; you got used to strange noises in an old house like this. The previous owners hadn't stayed there long, which seemed odd after going to all the effort of renovating it. Probably did it for the money: the house had come at a price. The Berridges had only moved there a year or so ago themselves—a last-ditch attempt to bandage an ailing marriage, a distraction, like trying for another baby: *perhaps we'll feel different about each other in a different house…*

Elaine scrolled through meaningless posts, cries for attention and boasts, without taking anything in. She struggled to concentrate and had a not unfamiliar sensation that she was being watched. She looked around the room, then sniffed the air. Whiskey. She'd smelt it before. No wonder, Pastor Carbonara had slipped into the room. He was perched on the arm of the other sofa, observing her. He liked to watch Elaine.

Like all of the ghosts, the pastor had died here on the premises. Tortured by lifelong celibacy, he had fled to England from New York, intending to renounce his faith. He never did, not really, merely retired; thus giving him the green light to indulge in the things that had been denied to him, namely liquor and women. The Cuckoo Inn had been just the place.

A chronic sot, especially towards the end, he had drunk himself to death in this very room. Keeled over and never woke back up. Died full of booze, and still acted that way now—hence the heavy step on the stairs, the reek of whiskey. He was emotional, up and down, a hopeless romantic. With slicked-back hair, grey at the sides, and a large silver cross dangling between the lapels of his jacket, he had the suave look of a 'wise guy' about him. Cordingley called him The Godfather; a joke that—like most of his—was lost on his fellow spirits.

The pastor held the marriage vow sacred, and though Elaine was off-limits, he still had a soft spot for her. She was lost and he wanted to save her. He prayed for her. *A confession would do her the world of good*, he thought. If only she would indulge him. As he looked on, Elaine glanced up at the clock on the wall and sighed. *He* would be home soon...

****

Shortly, a car pulled up on the drive at the front of the house. Elaine scuttled into the kitchen to check on dinner, to look busy. The front door opened and Hugh Berridge stepped into the hallway. He closed the door, put his briefcase down, then paused for a moment. He could hear sounds from the kitchen. She would have heard him come back. Who would say 'hi' first? *Leave it a moment*, he thought. Test the water. He popped his head into the lounge in the vain hope that one of the children might be downstairs. Fat chance. The lounge was empty. He remembered when he used to get greeted at the door by squeals of excitement, a *'Daddy's home!"* and a peck on the cheek. The pastor gave him a resigned two-fingered salute from the sofa as if to say, 'I know the feeling, compadre', then went back to watching the news.

Hugh made his way into the kitchen. Monotone 'hellos' and the briefest of eye contact were exchanged. As had become a habit, he made his way straight to the fridge for a cold can of beer. It was a defence, a sedative; it made things easier. Elaine watched out of the corner of her eye as he cracked the can open, his once athletic frame now paunched, his hair noticeably thinning. Still a handsome man, though, she begrudgingly accepted.

Hugh wanted to ask what was for dinner but knew better. Any question was a potential minefield, a trigger for an

15

explosion. Get the wrong one and a buzzer would sound '*Eeeehhh!*' and a trapdoor would open beneath his feet. Game over. But he was running out of options these days; even a 'How's your day been?' could open up a can of worms.

So they circled each other instead, each keeping their distance. Like two boxers in a ring. He moved towards the oven, she instinctively shifted towards the sink. He peered into the pan of peas, wanting to open up the oven to look inside but didn't dare. It was winding Elaine up. "Have I got time for a shower?" he asked. A feeler question, pretty harmless.

"Not really. It'll be ready in a minute." He took a long swig of beer, Dutch courage.

"What have we got?"

"Frozen crap." *Go on, say something. I dare you to say something*, she thought.

He didn't. He could tell it was one of those nights, so he shuffled off to the lounge to watch the sports news. Once there, with the TV on, he looked at the sports headlines on his phone instead.

"Dinner!" Elaine hollered up the stairs. It sounded more like a challenge than an invitation. Hugh was first up. Best not to antagonise her unnecessarily. He helped to bring the plates to the table, whilst fighting the urge to get another beer; a can of lager at the dinner table wasn't a good example to set to the children.

A few minutes later, it was still only Hugh and Elaine sitting at the table… or so they thought. All but three of the ghosts had trundled in to join them, led, as usual, by the younger ones, Sam first. There was something about dinner being called that made them come running. They liked to watch, to torment themselves. Sam would practically salivate at the sight of the family tucking in. He had a permanent emptiness in his belly.

In direct contrast, Cordingley couldn't bear the sight of food, or of it being eaten; it reminded him of the 'incident'. It had happened during the time of the Cuckoo Inn's failed reinvention as a gastropub. He had been tucking into a particularly succulent piece of John Dory when a rogue bone had got lodged in his throat. A colleague he had been lunching with had performed the Heimlich manoeuvre on him, successfully ejecting the offending item, but too late. Cordingley's body went limp in his arms, his face blue. He was laid on the floor in the same room that the Berridges now use as their dining room. Hence, Cordingley made himself scarce at mealtimes.

Colonel Pine, the matriarch of the group—a dapper gentleman with a military air about him and the regal elegance of a peacock—was the last to join them. Like Mrs Berridge, he enjoyed an afternoon siesta. Too proud to rush, he strolled into the dining room, dressed in tweed attire, a pocket watch attached to his waistcoat, a silver moustache and beard. The group instinctively stood up straighter when he entered. He acknowledged them with his cane.

The teenagers were still nowhere to be seen. Elaine opened her mouth to shout again, but Hugh couldn't bear another screech. "I'll go," he said, getting up from the table. This was a familiar routine, and a game Sam loved to play. He shot upstairs and, by the time Hugh had reached the landing, was already standing outside Leah's room. Hugh always turned left and made for Jake's room first, as he needed more rousing. At the same time as he knocked on

Jake's door, saying, "Jake, dinner," Sam knocked on Leah's door.

Hugh returned to the landing. "Leah, dinner!" Leah's door opened straightaway.

"Okay, I heard you the first time," she said as she emerged, clutching her phone.

"Oh, 'hi, Dad'," Hugh said. Leah looked up from her phone for a second to give him a sarcastic smile, before heading downstairs ahead of him.

Once Jake had finally slouched into the dining room, Elaine said, "It's probably cold now."

"Umm, waffles!" said Jake, without a hint of sarcasm, picking one up in his hands.

"Jake. Use a knife and fork, please," said Elaine. Leah picked at her food with a fork, whilst prodding away at her phone. "And can you put that away whilst we're at the table, young lady?" Leah tutted.

"So, how's everyone's day been?" said Hugh. He adopted a slightly higher-pitched, jovial voice when around the children that got on Elaine's nerves: an attempt at happy families. And his face didn't have that hangdog look about it, as if two invisible wires that had been pulling his face downwards had been snipped. Jake grunted through a mouthful of food in response, possibly a 'fine'. It was hard to tell.

"Yeah, great," said Leah. "Except I had to walk home in the rain."

"Really, how come?" said Hugh.

"Mum forgot to pick me up. She was asleep as usual."

Elaine stopped eating to glare at her daughter. "Leah. I've already apologised twice. You don't need to keep going on about it. You ought to try getting up at the crack of dawn to look after sick people. It's exhausting!"

"Oh well, the exercise probably did you good," said Hugh, trying to diffuse the situation.

"Hardly. I think I've got pneumonia. I don't know why we had to move out here to the middle of bloody nowhere anyway."

"It's hardly the middle of nowhere, Leah. It's a village, that's all."

"Well, it might as well be. None of my friends lives here, they're all in town. And catching the bus sucks."

"Please may I leave the table?" said Jake, getting up. He'd already wolfed his dinner down. It had taken all of two minutes.

"Can I be excused too?" said Leah.

"You've barely eaten anything," said Elaine.

"I'm not really hungry." Leah got up with her plate and her phone.

"Honestly, I don't know why I bloody bother," said Elaine.

The sound of plates being scraped into the bin could be heard from the kitchen. "Thanks," said Jake, passing back through. Leah followed, glued to her phone.

"Do you want to watch a film or something tonight, you two?" called Hugh.

"No, thanks," Jake replied.

"Leah?"

"I'm not watching another one of your '80s' films, Dad. We've seen them all a hundred times."

"Haven't you got homework, Jake?" Elaine called.

"Yeah, I'll do it in a bit!"

"Monopoly?" Hugh tried. The sound of their footsteps retreated up the stairs.

Hugh and Elaine looked at each other, then went back to their food. A heavy silence descended as both of their attempts at keeping their children downstairs failed. Elaine gave up on her dinner and got up from the table. She wasn't hungry either. Hugh was left to finish his dinner alone.

Alone, except for the ghosts. They watched him sadly. Some looked at each other and shook their heads. Things were getting worse; something had to be done.

Hugh sympathised with Leah to some extent about where they lived; he couldn't walk out of the door to the pub of an evening like he used to. Living in town, he used to have four on his doorstep. The only pub in this village was closed—and he resided in it. It had always been a dream—to run a pub, same with most men. Living in one had seemed the next best thing. The building still had some of its old features, some peculiarities—a cellar, a stable block, fireplaces in all of the bedrooms, a built-in safe, and a serving hatch from the kitchen up to the landing. It was as if the renovators had run out of money; that or they'd run into too many obstacles. The pub was a listed building. People were envious of the large, ivy-covered property; a sweeping driveway with a well in the front garden and pretty, diamond-hatched leaded windows; even those weren't allowed to be changed. Nice to look at, but they let in one hell of a draft.

No, living in a pub wasn't the same as going to one: the atmosphere, the company, the creamy head on a pint, a bit of banter with the landlord at the bar. Hugh sighed and got up from the table. Guess it will be another can from the fridge then…

Once he had left the room, Colonel Pine whispered, "Right, house meeting tonight at nine o'clock. Where are the others?"

"Did I hear a house meeting being mentioned?" said Cordingley, slipping into the room.

"Yes, you did," said the colonel, without elaborating.

"Paul's probably moping about somewhere, I expect," said Penny.

"Sam, go and find him. And wake that mulatto up. Actually, no. Let her sleep. She's always in a bad mood if you wake her before dark—she's like a damn vampire."

"You shouldn't call her that," said Juniper.

"What? A vampire?"

"No, that other thing."

"Why not? That's what she is—a mulatto." Juniper looked exasperated.

"Maybe in your day," chipped in Cordingley. "But in current parlance, the term is considered offensive—it says so on Wikipedia."

"Well, coloured then."

"You can't say that either."

"Oh, zip it, Cordingley."

Chapter Two

Later that evening, the ghosts were assembled in the stable block—more of an outbuilding these days. Where once it had been home to fine horses—the steeds of gentlemen, highwaymen and travellers—now it was full of junk. Sam still liked it in there; he felt at home. But he missed the hay, the smell of the horses, their warmth, and the steam from their nostrils. It was in his blood.

Meetings were always held in the stable block, away from the house. A gaggle of ghosts could kick up quite a racket, even just talking. And meetings had been known to get pretty heated. Everyone was present, except for Calypso. "Where is that damned girl?" said the colonel, tapping his cane impatiently.

"Probably making herself look beautiful," said the pastor.

"My ears are burning," said Calypso, appearing through the wall.

"Can't you use a door like any normal human being? It's undignified, springing out of nowhere like that," said the colonel.

"Oh, I'm sorry, honey bee. Did I scare you?" Calypso purred rather than spoke. There was something feline about her in general. A crepuscular ghost by habit, she slinked about when darkness fell, a former employee when the pub doubled as a brothel—one of the girls: the highest earner back in the day. Much sought after and requested due to her striking looks—a head of bushy hair, curvaceous figure, sensuous, full lips and irresistible milky coffee complexion; a natural flirt, and expert at making men happy.

She cast her eyes over the rest of the group. The twins were braiding each other's hair. Leofwine was off in a corner, scratching for mice. Cordingley was scratching his arms in his white short-sleeved shirt and tie; he suffered from chicken skin, and also had unfortunate protruding elbows that resembled golf balls. Sam was sitting cross-legged, stifling a yawn. "Still up, young Sam," Calypso said, bending down to tousle his hair. Sam's face lit up. He thought there was something exotic and fabulous about Calypso. And like most of the men present, his eyes were drawn to the front of her low-cut bodice, designed to show off her prize assets. Her 'coconuts', as she called them. They quivered and wobbled like jelly, seemingly with a life of their own. The pastor felt no shame in looking; he saw them as a gift from God. Cordingley twitched at the sight of them; he had an overwhelming desire to scoop them out with warm spoons and lather them with soap. The only male who averted his gaze was Paul Bearer; he was strictly a one-woman man.

"Of course he's up. This concerns him. It concerns all of us," said Penny, wanting to get down to business, fully aware of the distraction Calypso presented. "Things aren't getting any better. I worry for the family, for us."

"I agree," said the pastor. "You know how I feel about the D-word. It can't happen; they'll be cast out. Unsaveable. Damned!"

23

"We need to act quickly, make a pre-emptive strike," said the colonel.

"But what do you suggest? They don't communicate with each other anymore, the lot of them. I blame the gadgets," said Penny.

"You always blame the gadgets. You can't hold back technology!" said Cordingley.

"But they've ruined everything. All of them sitting there like zombies"—the pastor made the sign of the cross—"glued to their own screen, not speaking."

"He had his in the shower earlier," said Calypso. "Doing that thing again—'*shucking the corn!*'" She performed a brief but graphic demonstration with her right hand. Absinthe giggled. Juniper hit her. Sam looked confused. The colonel groaned and turned away in disgust.

"Men!" exclaimed Penny.

"What? She's just as bad! That thing she keeps locked in the safe," said Calypso.

"Sam, cover your ears," said Penny.

"Why don't they take pleasure in each other instead? They're married, it's not a sin," said the pastor.

"I don't know. It's sad. I took the batteries out of that thing once, but she just put new ones in," said Absinthe.

"Please, can we just stick to the point?" said the colonel. "Why does the tone always get lowered when Calypso's about? It's sex, sex, sex with you, isn't it?"

"Sex makes the world go around, sugar."

"Not in this house it doesn't," scoffed Penny.

"Enough!" said the colonel, banging his cane on the floor. There was silence for a moment.

"Well, I say again, what do you suggest? We've tried turning the whatsit off, the box thing," said Penny.

"The router, it's called a router," said Cordingley.

"Yes, that thing. And look at the trouble it caused—anyone would have thought we'd taken away their oxygen supply! And then there was the time Absinthe hid the gadget chargers—all hell broke loose."

Paul Bearer spoke for the first time. "I know what it's like to lose a loved one." There was a collective groan at this typical offering from the former funeral director.

"No one's died, man," said the colonel.

"No, but the love is dying. The people they were, the way they felt—they need to get it back. A change of scenery, a holiday perhaps. Somewhere they can reconnect. All of them."

"He might be on to something, you know," said the colonel, stroking his moustache. "A holiday could be just the thing. Somewhere they can't use the gadgets."

"What about that cottage they went to last year? Where was it—the Lake District?" said Penny.

"The Peak District, actually. They've been there dozens of times," said Cordingley.

"Thank you, Cordingley, for correcting me again; much appreciated," Penny grimaced. "Well, they came back from there moaning about the lack of Wi-Fi and phone signal."

"How's that going to help then?" said Juniper.

"Well, they obviously enjoy it if they keep going back there."

"But, how do we make it happen?" said Absinthe.

"Never underestimate the power of suggestion," said the colonel. "As Penny pointed out, we can't go charging in; it always ends in tears. A subtle hint here, a reminder there. Psychological warfare, see—propaganda. Maybe one of those e-mail things—Cordingley, that's your forte." Cordingley nodded smugly. "In the meantime, everyone must remain vigilant. I think we all ought to be assigned a family member to work on. There are four of them, nine of us. The twins count as one, so two to a person."

"I'll take Elaine under my wing," said the pastor. "I'll pray for her."

"I'll take Leah," piped up Sam, finding his voice, then blushing.

"Well, if we're all choosing, I'll have a man, any man," said Calypso. The colonel tutted.

"Wait, wait. Slow down. Who are we most worried about?" said Penny.

A chorus of 'Elaine' went up.

"She has an aura about her, a darkness. I fear for her," said Paul.

"He's right. I've noticed it too," said Juniper.

"Right, the twins and Carbonara—you're Elaine. Juniper, work some of your magic," said the colonel. The twins squealed and performed an impromptu pat-a-cake routine with each other.

"I'll make her one of my baths!" cried Juniper.

"Sam and Penny, you've got Leah. Penny, keep an eye on both of them! Myself and Paul will take the boy. Calypso, Cordingley, you've got Hugh." Calypso tutted at her choice of partner. "And any technological issues, report to Cordingley. That's it. Good luck. Meeting dismissed… Sam, get to bed!"

****

That night, under the light of a silvery moon, the twins set off for the ancient wood behind the house. There was more spectral traffic at night, but little or no human traffic; it wouldn't do for flowers and herbs to be plucked by an invisible hand, and placed into a basket, hovering in mid-air. Leofwine watched them leave through the fence at the bottom of the garden, Juniper in her white lace dress, Absinthe in black, both raven-haired. He mewled his displeasure at their departure.

Ghosts are usually bound to a particular place, whether it be a property, its perimeters, or tracts of land. In the twins' case, it was the wood in which they were hanged and the fields that surrounded it. When they'd died, being the eldest of the ghosts, this had encompassed the land that Cuckoo House now stood on; a source of envy to some of the other ghosts, as it meant the twins were free to roam the farthest. The house itself had had a colourful past: once acting as a temporary school during the Great War, and once being directly connected to a funeral parlour next door. An unscrupulous former landlord and equally immoral funeral director (not Paul Bearer) had negotiated a lucrative deal for wakes between themselves.

The twins were hanged a week apart: Juniper for alleged witchcraft, Absinthe for associating with a witch, refusing to denounce her sister or to acknowledge the powers that condemned her. It was quite rare at the time for a folk healer, especially one so young, to be accused of witchcraft; they were usually left well alone. But Juniper was still learning her trade. A botched remedy, containing beetroot juice amongst

27

other things, had caused the preacher's wife to break out in a rash, and to pass pink urine. The villagers had thought she'd been poisoned and was bleeding to death.

The ever-present Leofwine hadn't helped Juniper's cause; he followed her everywhere. Black as soot, and possessing odd-coloured eyes—one electric blue, the other lime green—a sure sign of a witch's familiar if ever there was one. *'Witchcraft!'* had been the cry. Despite being subjected to the pilnie-winks and the caspie-claws, as Absinthe looked on in horror, begging her sister to confess, Juniper had refused. She was hanged. Loyal to the end, Absinthe suffered a similar fate. Leofwine was drowned in what used to be the village well, poor thing.

From the woodland, the banks of the stream, the hedgerows and meadows, the twins located and picked herbs and plants that your average person wouldn't even know existed, yet had been there for centuries; hyssop, agrimony, and Juniper's favourite, mugwort—the witch's herb—for dreams; she said an incantation as she plucked it. Stinging nettle for circulation, wild hops for sleepfulness, dandelion and meadowsweet. On their wanderings, they bumped into other spirits from time to time, but nodded no more than a 'hello'; this wasn't a social outing, it was business.

Returning to the garden, Leofwine was waiting for them. There, they picked rosemary, mint and sage for ventilation, a bundle of lavender for calming the nerves, and calendula, orange blossom and rose petals for relaxation and fragrance. With their small basket full, they slipped back into the house. From the pantry, Juniper added cinnamon, ginger, lemon and honey. It was time to cook.

Juniper had made herbal baths and teas for Elaine before, but nothing this powerful; this was going to be a bomb. After asking Absinthe to close the doors and keep watch, she placed a large pan on the stove. This, she filled with two pints of milk and brought it up to a simmer. Once removed from the heat and allowed to cool slightly, one by one, she began to place the herbs, plants and flowers into it. She stirred them gently with a wooden spoon, allowing them to wilt and infuse. A wonderful, ambrosial smell filled the kitchen. Juniper looked at Absinthe and bit her lip. Absinthe giggled.

The concoction was left to cool. Once done, it was strained into a jug and everything was cleared up and put away, the wilted herbs buried in the compost heap. The special potion was hidden behind the loose wooden panel on the side of the bath; no mere bath milk for Cleopatra—this was nectar from the pagan gods!

Chapter Three

The next morning Cordingley was doing his J. Edgar Hoover bit. He always kept an eye on the family's technological activities—text messages, e-mails, internet use. Snooping was his thing; he even knew their individual passwords and usernames off by heart. But since the meeting, as the colonel had requested, he'd upped the ante. And it wasn't long before this vigilance paid off.

With Elaine at work, and the kids already at the bus stop, Hugh was eating his breakfast alone: the usual routine. He was prodding at his mobile, checking the sports news, when a text message came through from an unfamiliar number. Cordingley instinctively moved in, peering over Hugh's shoulder as he went to check it. The text read: '*Hey, Huey. Any chance u can give me a lift this Friday. Car's in the garage. x*'. Cordingley's eyebrows rose. The text wasn't from Elaine; her name would have come up. Besides, he'd never heard her call him 'Huey'. Ever. A sister, perhaps? No, he didn't have a sister. And a kiss—from a mystery woman.

Cordingley watched with interest as Hugh appeared to consider for a moment, staring out of the front window. He picked up the phone as if to reply, then put it back down. Sighing, he took a spoonful of cornflakes. After chomping and chewing for an age—the cornflakes were too dry: the kids had used all the bloody milk as usual—he picked up the phone again. Still chewing, he began to type. Cordingley leant in closer. Hugh rubbed at his neck, just above his shirt collar. Cordingley backed off a little. '*Can do. What time?*' he wrote, then wiped his palms on his trouser legs, as if sending the text had caused him to sweat.

After another mouthful of cornflakes, the phone lit up. '*8:15. Cheers hon. C u lata. xx*' Two kisses this time! And 'hon'—clearly short for honey. What was this woman, some kind of floozy? There was no name, which was infuriating. Hugh didn't react in any way, didn't even reply. He did, however, promptly delete both texts from his phone. Cordingley put a fist in his mouth to stifle a gasp. Suspicious. *Highly* suspicious.

Hugh got up from the table, left his phone, gave his breakfast pots a rinse, and then headed upstairs to brush his teeth. Cordingley waited till he heard the landing creak, then reached for the phone. He pressed the button on the side of it and the screen lit up. Swiping it, he went straight to messages and began to scroll down. There were hundreds of them. Hugh wasn't in the habit of deleting messages, nor did he have a password on his phone, which made the fact that he had deleted those two recent messages even more suspicious. Cordingley kept scrolling, his eyes beadily scanning for texts without contact names, opening them up, and then moving on.

He heard the toilet flush upstairs; he was running out of time. Faster and faster he went. Just then, a number flashed past that looked familiar, ending in the digits 1 and 4. He went back to it. The message began with the words: '*Hey, Huey*'. He opened it up. '*Hey, Huey. Don't forget audit today. Dawn,*

31

accounts'. The message was sent a month or so ago. There were footsteps descending the stairs. Cordingley quickly closed the phone down. But it was still lit up when Hugh entered the room, pulling his suit jacket on. He went straight over to the table, expecting a further text. Nothing. He made a puzzled expression, tucked the phone in his jacket pocket, and then left for work.

Cordingley raced upstairs. He couldn't wait to tell the colonel—to tell everyone, in fact. He felt important, needed, part of the group. "Wake up! Everybody wake up! I've got some important news!"

Despite being up most of the night, the twins were already on the landing, giggling. *Lord knows what there was to giggle about at this time of the morning*, thought Cordingley, as he passed them, banging on doors and walls. Groans could be heard from various rooms. It was early. Ghosts were seldom early risers, especially the older ones. For Cordingley, it was still a habit to get up for work. Sam popped his head out of the serving hatch; he was hiding from the twins, playing hide-and-seek. He hid in there every time, and the twins always pretended not to know where he was.

One by one, the ghosts appeared, all except for Calypso. The colonel was the last to emerge, his normally immaculate hair a little skew-whiff, none too pleased about being disturbed. He'd just nodded back off, comfortable in the recently vacated marital bed. Cordingley saluted him. "I've made an important interception, Colonel!"

"Bit early for football, isn't it, Cordingley?" said the pastor, wryly. The twins and Sam, who'd climbed out of the serving hatch to join them, sniggered.

"Yes, at ease, Cordingley. We're not at war… thankfully. An interception, you say?"

"Affirmative. At 0800 hours"—the colonel gave him a withering look with raised eyebrows—"Sorry, about ten minutes ago. A text message to Mr Berridge, two of them, in fact, from…" He paused for effect. "A mystery woman." The ghosts began to pay attention.

"A mystery woman, contacting our Mr Berridge? Who is this trollop?" said Penny protectively.

"Well, after some intensive detective work, scouring Mr Berridge's device—the Samsung Galaxy Mini S5—"

"Get to the point, Cordingley," said the colonel.

"Quite. I came across another text, a month or so ago, from the same number—a woman by the name of Dawn."

The pastor let out a cry and made the sign of the cross. "Adultery! That explains it, poor Elaine!" Paul Bearer's shoulders slumped in response.

"Wait, Pastor. Let's not jump to conclusions. We don't know that yet," said Penny.

"Well, what did the message say? What did any of them say?" asked Juniper.

"The first one seemed fairly routine, a work thing, something about an audit. But the second one was a request for a lift to work this Friday. Apparently, this woman's car is in the garage. Or so she claims."

"So, what's the big deal? There's nothing suspicious in that. All seems pretty innocent to me," said the colonel.

"Did he reply?" asked Penny. The ghosts leant in, hanging on Cordingley's answer.

"Yes, he replied. He said he would give her a lift." A few gasps rose up.

"Well, it still doesn't mean anything. Just a favour for a work colleague, that's all," said Penny, desperate to give Hugh the benefit of the doubt.

"Oh, there's more, I'm afraid," said Cordingley.

"More?" groaned Paul.

"Yes. More. She was very familiar with him, calling him Huey and Honey, and—I hate to say this—even signed the texts with kisses." The pastor sunk to his knees, muttering a Hail Mary. There were murmurs all around. "Not only that. He deleted the texts afterwards… Mr Berridge never deletes his texts." The pastor was rolling around now, wailing, as if a stake had been driven through his heart.

"And did he return any of this familiarity, this vulgar, misplaced affection in any way?" asked the colonel.

"No. In Mr Berridge's defence, I can't say that he did."

"Women always use kisses on messages these days. Leah does it all the time—and Elaine. I've seen them. It doesn't mean anything anymore," said Juniper.

"Well, there you go!" said Penny. "I'm not surprised he deleted the texts. This trollop, this office floozy, is trying to get her hooks into him, a married man no less—she must be stopped!"

"When is this secret rendezvous taking place again?" asked the colonel.

"This coming Friday, before work."

"Well, we must put a stop to it—or at least put a spanner in the works. It's the last thing we need right now. Any ideas, anyone?"

"I do," said Absinthe. "Let's make him smell. No woman likes a man who smells!" Sam gave a sniff of his armpit.

"How can we make him smell? Mr Berridge always smells so fresh," said Penny.

"Oh, there are many ways to make a man smell, aren't there, sis?" Absinthe took Juniper's hand. "Come on." And they toddled off.

"Now, hold on. Mr Berridge is my jurisdiction!" cried Cordingley.

"Trust us, Cordingley, you don't want to get involved in this!" Juniper called over her shoulder. Sam got up and trotted after them in curiosity. Whatever they were up to, it sounded like fun.

The rest of the group watched them go. It was always more interesting when the young ones were around. They brought a bit of life to proceedings. "Anyone else got anything to report?" sighed the colonel.

"Nothing of note," said the pastor, getting back to his feet, a little shamefaced at his histrionics.

Paul shook his head.

"Leah's spending far too much time on those silly websites as usual," said Penny. "Writing some pretty sombre things, actually. I think she's lonely. I might see if I can dig out some old photos today, some holiday snaps at the cottage and that."

"And I'm going to have a little meddle with Mr Berridge's laptop," said Cordingley.

Meanwhile, downstairs, the twins had removed a handful of choice, juicy prawns from the freezer. These were promptly defrosted in warm water, then placed in the greenhouse under a hot sun to ripen for a few days. Then they set off over the fields to locate a prime specimen of dog muck. Sam stood at the fence and watched enviously, stroking Leofwine.

****

That evening, after dinner, the Berridge children couldn't wait to retreat to their rooms. A row had been building between their parents, and they didn't want to be around when it broke. Jake turned his rap music up, so he didn't have to listen to it, and lost himself in killing things and blowing things up. Leah returned to her tablet. Ooh, three new notifications from Facebook, two of them friend requests. *Goody*, she thought. None all week, then two come together. She liked collecting friends; it was a bit of a competition at school—see who could get the most. To this end, she rarely discriminated. Accepted anyone really.

The first one was from a dorky girl in her year, Lucy O'Brien—'Loser Lucy'. Leah clicked accept. '*You can now see Lucy's friends and posts*'. No, thanks. Moving on, the other one was much more interesting. A boy. Her heart fluttered. She didn't recognise his name, nor his face from the thumbnail. She clicked accept. '*You can now see Ryan's friends and posts*'. Yes, please. Leah opened up his profile, made his face bigger. Ryan Daniels. Nice picture. He was fit. About the same age as her, perhaps a little older. His hair was short at the sides, as was the fashion, and he was wearing a red baseball cap with a football badge on it. He looked a bit like Justin Beiber. She still didn't recognise him, though. Perhaps he was in the year above.

Leah briefly scanned his details. Born 2002. Yes, a year older. Funny, she hadn't seen him about. *Ah, that's why*, she thought, he went to the other school—the posh one, King's. Strange that he was friend requesting her then. Something to brag about anyway. She went to check out his friends, to see if there were any mutual ones, but his privacy settings wouldn't allow it. Oh well, she sighed.

Moving on again, Leah checked out the other notification. She had been tagged in a picture… by her mother of all people. "God, I wish she wouldn't do that!" she said out loud. It had been a condition of Leah having a Facebook account that her parents were friends with her—to keep an eye on her. Her dad never bothered with it, but her mum was getting embarrassing, especially with all the depressing stuff she'd been posting lately. Leah clicked on the post, dreading what it was going to be—something mortifying no doubt.

It was a cringe-worthy holiday photo of the whole family at the cottage in Derbyshire. They were standing on the farm gate, wearing wellies. *I wonder who took the photo*, she mused. Must have been one of the Fletchers. They all looked so young, especially Jake. He had changed so much. Even Mum and Dad looked younger and happier. Probably drunk. She smiled despite the humiliation. Dad had his arm around Mum. *Can't remember the last time I saw that*, she thought sadly. *And oh, my God! I'm wearing a High School Musical sweatshirt! And look at my frizzy hair! Right, it's getting deleted.* Her nostalgia quickly vanished and teenage self-consciousness returned. She deleted the post, hoping no one had seen it. Too late. Someone had commented on it. '*Nice sweatshirt!*' *Damn*, Leah thought. *Mum can't keep on doing this. I'm going to have to defriend her. Would she be hurt if I did?*

Already bored with Facebook, Leah moved onto Instagram.

The watching Penny gave a nod to Sam. Sam gave her a thumbs-up back and left the room. He was to inform

Cordingley that the picture had been seen. Cordingley then had the small matter of deleting the post from Elaine's account to deal with before she saw it.

Chapter Four

"Goodnight, Miss Collins. See you in the morning."

"Night, Mrs Price. See you tomorrow."

Being head librarian, Mrs Price insisted on addressing colleagues formally, and vice versa. It gave the library the air of an educational institute, which it was really: a place for learning. Sadly, though, it was a dying institute. Thirty years she'd been there. Worked her way up to the top. It was shocking how things had changed in that time. She was old-fashioned, once formidable; her 'hush' for silence had been legendary. Now there was no need to hush anyone; the library was silent most of the time. People just didn't borrow books anymore; it was all Kindles and e-books. Even the children only came in to use the computers.

Mrs Price sighed as she crossed the empty library to shut the door properly and lock it. There was a time when she practically had to boot them out at closing time. *No doubt libraries would soon go the way of the record shops, the local banks and post offices*, she thought. Obsolete. She watched Miss Collins through the glass as she walked away, with that strange gait of hers. A decent enough sort, a little slovenly perhaps—blouse always a little creased, and often a whiff of body odour about her; especially towards the end of the week.

It was unbecoming in a woman. But how does one broach such a thing with a person? She could do with losing some weight. No wonder she hadn't married…

Miss Collins caught the bus home. She disembarked at her stop and made the short walk down the terraced street where she lived. She couldn't wait to get her shoes off; they were killing her. As if on cue she stumbled, jarring her ankle, as one of her heels got caught in a crack between the paving slabs. "*Shit!*"

She pulled her keys out of her handbag and unlocked the front door. One of her nails was cracked, she noticed. The smell that greeted her from inside the house was both rank and welcoming at the same time. "Aah, home," she said, drinking it in.

The second the door was closed to the outside world, Miss Collins kicked off her shoes and pulled off the mousy brown wig she wore. It had been driving her mad all the way home. "Thank fuck for that," she said, scratching at the pool ball tattoo on her shaved head. She dumped the wig on the floor, then struggled to unzip her skirt at the back; it was tight as hell around her stocky midriff. Sucking in her stomach, the zip eventually gave and she stepped out of the skirt. Then she threw off her blouse to reveal more tattoos at the top of her arms.

She stood in the hallway in black tights and some serious hold-me-in underwear—more like a corset or a plate of armour than underwear. This came off too, along with the tights. It was a blessed relief. "Aah, that's better." She smelt ripe underneath—sweaty, fishy. Again, it was somehow comforting, familiar. She padded down the hallway in a bra and boxer shorts, scratching her backside, more tattoos on her back and calves. A pit bull in makeup.

Miss Collins made straight for the lounge, a sea of pizza boxes, dirty plates, cups and junk. In the middle of it, a filthy, brown sofa. She reached underneath it to pull out one of her many laptops. Firing up the laptop, she reached for her tobacco tin on the coffee table and sunk back onto the sofa. She lifted her leg to break wind and then proceeded to roll a fag. The cracked false nail was hanging off, hampering her. She pulled it off to reveal a stubby, sunken-in fingernail underneath. She felt like pulling them all off. But she had one more day to the weekend. Then she could.

After lighting her roll-up, she tapped a few buttons on the laptop then got back up. She located some dirty grey jogging bottoms and a baggy T-shirt amongst the junk and put them on. Lastly, from the arm of the sofa, she plucked her beloved Manchester United cap and placed it snugly on her head. Now she was ready.

Plonking herself back down, fag in hand, hunched forward, she negotiated her way to Facebook. "Right, let's see what the catfish has caught today," she said. She always got a thrill, a pulse of excitement at this time, a building of anticipation. Like a fisherman reeling in his net, or a poacher checking his traps. "Aha! We've got some wrigglers," she said, rubbing her hands together. "Four of them." A good day. Once they'd accepted your friend request, you were in. She briefly checked them all out. One of them looked promising, local by the looks of it. A Leah Berridge.

After taking a wheeze on her fag, it was time to initiate phase two. She sent a message to Leah first. '*Hi*'. That was it; that's all it took. Reel them in, make them curious; let *them* do the work. You push too hard and they get suspicious. Slowly, slowly, catchy monkey—that was the way. She'd put in hours of graft before on individuals, only for them to slip through her cyber-fingers at the last minute. Only once had it come to fruition: an actual meeting. Contact.

After sending the same message to the three other girls, she returned to Leah. Phase three: research. "Let's have a good look at you, my pretty," she said, reopening Leah's profile. Firstly, she checked out her photos—the usual selfies, narcissistic poses. There didn't seem to be that many with friends. There were none with family at all. Status: single. This made her smile. She took another drag on her fag and clicked on 'More about Leah'. Hobbies—listening to music, playing the guitar. Likes Ed Sheeran, Jamie Lawson… could be useful. She went to Uppingham Academy in town. Lived in a village called Alderleigh, a mile or so out of town. Always whinging about it by the look of some of her posts. Used to live in town and walk to school. That could be it—a way in. She blew out smoke and stubbed out her fag.

****

Elaine was running a bath. Like Leah, she couldn't wait to disappear upstairs, to retire for the evening. A bath was a good excuse to be left alone. She checked the water, adjusted the taps, poured in some bath milk, then went to her bedroom to get undressed.

The twins had been waiting for this moment. Elaine didn't always have a bath, sometimes she showered. "Quick, Quick!" said Juniper to Absinthe. "Keep watch!" The second Elaine left the bathroom, Juniper pulled out her special potion

42

from behind the loose bath panel. She quickly emptied the entire jug into the bath, then hid the jug again. The same intoxicating smell that had filled the kitchen filled the bathroom. Juniper dipped her hand into the water to mix the potion in. "Ow! It's too hot!"

"Use the loo brush," said Absinthe.

"No! Gross!"

"Use a toothbrush then."

"Not big enough." She spied a plunger next to the sink. "That'll do." She turned it upside down, just in case, and stirred the bathwater around with the wooden end.

"Quick! She's coming! Put it back!"

Juniper replaced the plunger where she'd found it, but too quickly. It rocked back and forth on its hard rubber cup, in danger of toppling over. The twins watched, wide-eyed, as it righted itself, its wooden end still wet, just as the bathroom door opened. Elaine re-entered the bathroom, wrapped in a towel, another in her hand. The twins stood aside as she checked the temperature of the bath again. Leaving the cold tap running, Elaine paused for a moment before disrobing to sniff the steamy air. A dreamy look came over her face and she closed her eyes for a second, drinking in the heavenly vapour. The twins looked at each other and smiled. Juniper nodded towards the door. They slipped out, leaving Elaine to her bath.

****

Dressed in her pyjamas post-bath, a towel wrapped around her head, Elaine lay in bed in the dark. The sheets and duvet felt crisp and cool. In contrast, her body was glowing with heat. She felt an assault on her senses, both physically and mentally. A euphoria. A delightful languor—somehow alive yet sleepy at the same time. The only thing she could compare it to was the marijuana buzzes she used to get at university, or perhaps the residual afterglow of a good orgasm. Her sinuses were cleared, her stuffy summer cold gone. Her skin felt fresh and revitalised; it tingled. She tingled everywhere, a numbing tingle. In her private parts. They radiated warmth, buzzed. She felt horny, but weak as a kitten, considered touching herself, but felt too drowsy. Above all else, she felt drowsy…

Elaine dreamt of a time before she was married. She dreamt in black and white. She was a girl, a teenage girl. She was in love, with her first love; her first real relationship; her only relationship before her husband. It was a time of love letters, exchanging records via a go-between on the school bus, discovering sex, music and alcohol. She dreamt of his family's house, of the close that he lived on, sitting in the small, private back garden, surrounded by conifers. How his family had taken her in. The smell of furniture polish on a Saturday morning when she'd stayed over for the night. It was a haven, a utopia; she went to in her mind, and in her dreams; especially over the last year or so.

Safe in the cocoon of her bed, Elaine drifted in and out of sleep, not wanting the feeling to go, not wanting to leave that place. She wanted to stay there forever; so content, so warm…

Chapter Five

When Elaine awoke the next morning, it was like waking up underwater. Deep, deep water. Existence was a murky ocean, and she was at the bottom of it. The permanent, crushing weight of depression wanted to suffocate her, to extinguish her. She gasped for air and sobbed. But the dream wouldn't leave her. Remnants of it stayed with her. Like a brightly coloured balloon to hold onto in a grey world. She decided she was going to contact the boy, the man. She'd been meaning to for years. She'd already tracked him down on Facebook. But she was never alone. Never. During her break at work, she'd do it then.

Wrapped in a dressing gown, Elaine trudged to the bathroom. The twins, already awake on the landing, watched her walk past. She looked so sad. They shot downstairs to wake the pastor. He was fast asleep in his usual place—the sofa in the lounge. He'd asked them to wake him when Elaine got up. The previous evening, he and Penny had sorted out some choice holiday snaps of the cottage. These had been placed at the top of a pile of photos, strategically left on the coffee table in the lounge. Elaine always put the TV on first thing, whilst she had a coffee to wake herself up.

This morning was no different. Except that Elaine looked sadder than ever. Her aura was darker, her mood more sombre. She looked catatonic, a walking zombie, as she entered the lounge with her coffee. She placed her cup on the table right next to the pile of photos. The ghosts nudged each other expectantly, but Elaine didn't even notice the photos. Instead, she reached for the TV remote. She wrapped her dressing gown tighter around her, saying, "Bloody freezing," as she turned on the telly. She often talked to herself in the morning, and she often swore.

Elaine stared at the TV for a few moments with glazed eyes, then sat back on the sofa, tucking her legs to the side. As she reached for her coffee, her hand nudged the edge of the photo pile. But still, she didn't register them. She took a sip of coffee and reached into her dressing gown pocket for her phone. This was also a familiar routine. The ghosts looked at each other again, exasperated. Elaine continued to sip at her coffee and scroll through her phone with her thumb. The same motion, repeated over and over. This was exactly what they were talking about. What they hated.

Never one to shy away from being proactive, Absinthe got up from the sofa. She crouched down by the coffee table and waited. Elaine kept prodding with her thumb, then looking up, staring off into the distance from time to time, the coffee cup still cradled in her lap. Just when Absinthe was about to lose her patience—she felt like tipping the cup over Elaine and her phone—Elaine went to put the cup back. Absinthe waited till exactly the right moment, then nudged the photos, just enough to upset the pile. The photos slid across the coffee table, catching Elaine's attention. "Shit," she said. *What were they doing there?*

She went to tidy them up. Hugh getting sentimental, no doubt. He often did at night when he was drunk, going over old photos, sometimes old video footage. She couldn't be doing with it. She restacked the pile, with no intention of looking at the photos when the top one caught her eye. It was of the cottage they rented. A snow scene—the cottage and front garden covered in snow. All of them were standing next to a snowman they'd built. They'd put the timer on the camera, she remembered, propped it on a stepladder. It had taken ages to get it right. That would have been the New Year they'd spent there. They'd got snowed in—the lane up to the cottage anyway. They'd had to walk to the pub for food and drinks. Half of the pub was an Indian restaurant. They'd had curry on New Year's Day, just the four of them; it had been wonderful.

They'd spent Christmases there too. Elaine flicked to the next photo. There you go. A Christmas scene. All of them sitting around the large kitchen table, party hats on their heads. The Aga had been a nightmare to light: smoked them all out at first. But lovely when it had got going, warmed the kitchen up no end, the bedroom above it too. No one wanted to leave it. They'd stay up late, playing cards and drinking wine at the table. Happy days. She smiled. The Fletchers had joined them at a house in the village that year. What happened to the Fletchers? What happened to any of their friends?

There *was* something special about the place, though. Everyone relaxed there, unwound. Elaine flicked through a few more photos. Most of them seemed to be of the cottage. Long days, sunny days, spring days, Halloween. There weren't many seasons or many years, they hadn't been there. *Look at me getting sentimental now*, she thought. Perhaps that was his plan. Perhaps Hugh had left them there on purpose to suck her in. Well, it wasn't going to work. She'd seen enough. The little ray of sunshine they'd proffered, the brief respite from the grey, quickly disappeared.

Elaine was running late. She got up, taking her coffee cup and the photos with her. They could go back where they'd come from; that way there wouldn't be a conversation about them.

****

A few hours later Hugh was making his way to his car. It was a warm day, a Friday, the day he was meant to be giving Dawn a lift to work. The previous night the twins had been busy. The handful of raw prawns had been removed from the greenhouse. They were slimy, crawling with maggots, and stunk to high heaven. Sam had begged the twins to let him help. But when the smell hit him, he wished he hadn't. All three of them were retching as the prawns were scraped of maggots and spooned into a sandwich bag. The bag was tucked deep under the dark recesses of the front passenger seat of Hugh's car: a place where no human could see or reach. Sam's stick-thin arms were ideal for this. A few air holes were then jabbed into the bag with a pencil.

Next, it was the turn of Hugh's shiny work shoes. He always put them on in the porch, the last thing before leaving for work. The dog muck specimen that had been singled out for consistency was pasted onto the bottom of one of them. Using a knife, the dog muck had been spread and moulded like pate, wedged up against the inside of a heel. This way it would smell, but he wouldn't go treading it all over his car and car pedals. The ghosts could be Machiavellian, but they were thoughtful too.

As Hugh opened the car door, the smell hit him straightaway. "Jesus Christ!" he said, covering his nose and throwing his briefcase on the passenger seat. "What *is* that?" He was already feeling a little nervous about today, guilty even as if he was embarking on an affair. Who knows, perhaps he was. Perhaps this was fate. He sniffed around the interior, trying to locate where the stink was coming from. It was impossible; the smell seemed to be everywhere. Still covering his nose with his jacket, he wound down the driver's side window, then leant across and opened the passenger side one. That was slightly better. He checked the back seats, the floor, the side pockets, the seat pockets. Had one of the kids left a half-finished sandwich somewhere? Had a mouse crawled in and died? He checked under the front seats and rummaged as far as he could with his hand. He checked the glove compartment, the boot. Nothing. It was a mystery.

Tentatively, Hugh settled down into the driver's seat. He was going to be late. He started the car. Perhaps if he turned the fan on it would help. It didn't. Just circulated the smell further around the car, stirring it up. He turned the fan off again. Hopefully, driving with the windows down would help. He opened the rear ones too for good measure.

By the time he reached Dawn's house, he had got used to the smell a little. So in his mind, it had diffused, weakened. Not so for Dawn as she got in the car. Even the bottle of perfume she had dowsed herself in didn't mask it. Did she mention it or ignore it? She couldn't ignore it; it was making her gag. "God, Huey. What is that awful smell?"

Mr Berridge went bright red. "I don't know. It doesn't usually smell like this, I promise. I was hoping that perhaps it was outside, but it's definitely in the car. I've checked everywhere, though."

"It smells like dog muck."

"Dog muck? No, it's worse than that."

"No, I can definitely smell dog muck. Have you checked your shoes?"

"But I haven't been anywhere."

"Check them anyway."

Hugh tutted, left the car running and stepped out to check his shoes. This was embarrassing. Dawn rooted around in her handbag, whilst Hugh lifted one shoe up to check underneath it. Nothing. Why was he even bothering? He only used these shoes for work. Second shoe. Uggh, a substantial dollop of semi-firm dog shit. How the hell did that get there?

"What the hell? Gross!" Hugh reddened further and offered an awkward apologetic smile to Dawn. She was watching him from within the car, a tissue pressed against her nose. He began to search around for a stick. Finding one, he proceeded to prise off the offending clag. Dawn pulled a face and looked away. Once done, and feeling like an idiot, Hugh wiped his shoe backwards, forwards and sideways on a grassy bank. Satisfied but still feeling squeamish, he got back in the car. "Sorry about that."

But the smell remained. "It's still there," said Dawn, removing her tissue temporarily. "Worse!"

"Well, it's not me! I promise," he said, putting the car in gear. Why was she making such a big deal out of it? It was starting to annoy him. "Just ignore it." She gave him a look.

The smell did the trick—like the opposite of an aphrodisiac. It was hard to talk or think about anything else. Dawn tactfully negotiated a lift home with another work colleague, a female one. Hugh wasn't so lucky. The stench had increased and ripened during the day, making the journey home torturous.

Once back, he vowed to get to the bottom of it. He couldn't have another day like that tomorrow. Pulling up on the drive, he switched off the engine and opened all the car doors to let out the smell. Then he marched into the house to find some gloves and, hopefully, a mask. The look on his face pleased the ghosts, standing at the window, watching out for him. It looked as if their trick had worked. The second Hugh was in the house, prompted by the others, Sam slipped out to the car. He reached underneath the passenger seat and pulled out the stinking bag. Making sure the coast was clear, he ran to the bin at the side of the house with it, gagging all the way. The elder ghosts looked on nervously. The twins couldn't stop giggling. Hugh never got to the bottom of the smell. He left the car windows open overnight, and over the next few days, the stink disappeared entirely.

****

Hugh and Elaine were both in the lounge, mere feet from each other, but worlds apart. Elaine was on her phone; Hugh was firing up the family laptop, beer in hand. The TV was on, but neither of them was watching it. It was just white noise in the background to disguise the silence. There was nothing on anyway; there never was. Hugh thought he'd watch a couple of *Breaking Bad* episodes. He was really into it, but it wasn't Elaine's thing.

As the laptop came to life, a surprised look spread across Hugh's face, and he glanced over at Elaine. She had a glazed expression, staring at her phone, thumb going. Hugh looked back at the screen. Someone had changed the screensaver. It was a picture of them all at the cottage they rented in the Peak District. A nice one. They all looked happy. This made him sad, and he took a long draught of beer. *But who had changed it, Elaine? Perhaps she privately wanted to go but was too stubborn to say so. She did enjoy it there. She always unwound, was less uptight. Perhaps this was a hint.* It gave Hugh hope, a little glowing ember inside. He took another sip of beer for courage, already on his third can. "Elaine, did you change the screensaver on the laptop?" There was a boyish smile on his face.

Elaine didn't even look up. Her voice was the usual impassive monotone; "Why would I do that?" Then there was silence. Hugh felt crushed. The moment gone, the ember extinguished, just like that. He took another sip of beer.

"Oh, no reason." *Forget it*, he thought. Must have been one of the kids. He quickly moved on, negotiating his way to Netflix.

As he did so, an advert came up at the side of the screen. It happened all the while—targeted marketing enticements. But this one caught his eye. It was an advert for the cottage, from the company they rented it off. That was weird. He hadn't been browsing their site lately, which was when this sort of thing typically came up. It happened on his phone, too—constantly. And e-mails; they drove him mad. He clicked on the advert: '*Holywell Cottage. You rented this property on 23/05/15. Mini-break still available weekend 25/05/16'.* This was too much of a coincidence. He looked over at Elaine again. "Are you sure you haven't been on the laptop?"

She looked up this time, almost irritated. "When would I have had time to go on the laptop? I'm too busy cooking, or cleaning, or ironing." *Or asleep,* thought Hugh but didn't say anything.

"Well, someone has. They've changed the screensaver. Look." He went back to the home screen then turned the laptop around. *Oh, wow,* thought Elaine. *That's just sad. That's pathetic. First, he conveniently leaves photos of the cottage on the coffee table, then tries to draw my attention to it by changing the screensaver on the laptop—then questions me about it.* She gave him a withering look.

"I wouldn't even know how to change the screensaver on the laptop," she said. *Um, that's probably true,* Hugh thought.

"Well, it must have been one of the kids then," he said, turning the laptop back around and going back to the advert. "Perhaps they want to go." Elaine shook her head at his desperation and went back to her phone. He clicked on the availability button to look at the price of the cottage. "You didn't fancy it, did you?" There was still hope in his voice.

"Fancy what?" *Why did he keep bugging her?*

"The cottage. It's available May half-term."

Oh, there we go. There it is, thought Elaine. "Quite frankly, it's the last thing on my mind right now."

"Oh, come on. It will do us good—the kids, I mean. Get them away from their screens for a bit. They love it there."

"You mean *you* love it there! I'm sure they'll be thrilled with being stuck out in the middle of nowhere with no Wi-Fi at their age. Good luck with that one! We do the same things every time there. We've done it all to death. They're too old for it now."

This riled Hugh. It was as if she was picking apart everything he held sacred, all their memories there. "Or is it the lack of Wi-Fi that bothers *you* more?" he challenged, taking a swig of beer.

"I'm not even going to answer that."

The conversation was bordering on an argument now. But Hugh didn't want it to go that way, and he checked his anger. "I feel like we're losing them, Elaine."

"Look, if you want to book the cottage and play happy bloody families, then go ahead and book it! Just don't involve me!"

"I will!"

"Good!"

He would as well. Sod her. He began filling out the booking request form, his fingers shaking slightly. She'd given up, pure and simple. But he hadn't.

There. It was done. He pressed send. "And what do I tell them then? The kids. When they ask why you're not coming?"

"I don't know! That's your problem. Tell them their mother's suicidally depressed!"

He looked at her in despair, no longer angry, just deflated. "Perhaps one of those molten vindaloos at the pub near the cottage would cheer you up." It was his last effort at persuasion, humour, making the peace. Elaine didn't answer, she was scrolling through her phone again. Hugh got up to get another beer.

After cracking open his can, he went upstairs to tell the kids. Jake first. He had his music pounding out. Eminem. It was the weekend. Hugh knocked on his door before entering. Jake looked a little surprised. He turned the music down. "Hold on," he said into his mouthpiece, then took the headset off. "Hi," he said. His dad looked a little drunk.

"Hi. Hey, guess what? I've booked the cottage for a few days during the May half-term."

Jake's face was a picture, digesting the information. Forever the diplomat, the sensitive soul. "Er, how long for?" *Please don't say a week, please don't say a week*, he thought.

"Four days. Hopefully, anyway—I'm just waiting for confirmation."

"OK, cool. Can I take the Xbox?"

"Jake, that's not really the idea, is it?"

"But you guys go to bed earlier than I do—drunk normally—and I get bored!"

"I suppose so then. Night times only, though! That reminds me, did you change the screensaver on the laptop?"

"No, why?"

"Someone has. Have you been on the laptop at all today?"

"No, why?"

"No reason." *Must have been Leah then. Unless Elaine's bluffing*, Hugh thought. *Maybe she was planning on going to the cottage without him. Surely things hadn't gotten that bad, had they? But then why would she have changed the screensaver and drawn attention to it? That didn't make sense.* His thoughts were muddled by the beer. "Hey, did you want to come and watch a couple of *Breaking Bad*'s with me?"

"Maybe later." Jake put his headphones back on.

"OK."

Hugh knocked on Leah's door. "Leah, can I come in?" There was no answer. "Leah?" He pushed open the door. Leah was on her bed with her earphones in, tablet in hand. She jumped and looked guilty.

"Jesus, Dad. You scared me!" She covered her tablet with a pillow, Hugh noticed, and picked up her phone. She began moving her thumbs, her face flushed.

"Hi, what you up to?"

"Nothing, why?"

"I'm not accusing you. Just asking."

"Oh, just chatting with mates, listening to music."

"Take your earphones out a minute."

"It's OK, I've got the sound down, I can hear you."

"Just, take them out a minute; I want to talk to you." Leah pulled a face and removed one earphone. "Thank you. I was just telling Jake, I've booked the cottage for a few days during the half-term. I think it will do us all good to get away for a while." Unlike Jake, Leah wasn't good at hiding her feelings.

"Aaaaghh!" she groaned, sticking her face into her pillow.

"Hey! You used to love going to the cottage. You can go pony-trekking and"—she let out another groan at this, kicking her feet—"we can go on the cable cars…"

"But there isn't any Wi-Fi," Leah mumbled into her pillow.

Hugh snapped. "There's more to life than bloody Wi-Fi, you know! There's a whole world out there!" *Jesus, where had that come from*, thought Leah, realising she'd overstepped the mark.

But it wasn't just Leah, it was the whole damn lot of them, thought Hugh. Ungrateful sods and their precious bloody Wi-

Fi. He was sick of it. "Well, we're all going. And that's final. So you'd better get used to the idea!" He stormed out.

"OK! It's fine!" called Leah.

Leah's bedroom was right above the lounge. Elaine heard Hugh raising his voice and slamming the door. She pulled a 'told you so' face, clocked by the pastor, then went back to her phone. Penny had watched the conversation unfold from the corner of Leah's room. When Hugh had gone, she put her hands around Leah's neck, inches from her and made as if to strangle her violently. Little brat.

Once the coast was clear, Leah pulled her tablet back out. She'd been in the middle of a very important conversation. The boy, Ryan, had been messaging her on Facebook. That was why the thought of going away to the cottage was so horrific. Bad timing. '*Hi*' was all he had said at first. But it had given her a real thrill. She hadn't known how to answer and was going to just put 'Hi' back. But it seemed a bit dumb, a bit lacking in personality. Various replies had been typed, then deleted again; the modern-day equivalent of screwing up unsatisfactory love letters and throwing them into a wastepaper bin. In the end, she had put: '*Hi. How do you know me?*' Her heart had thumped louder with every letter typed; and when she pressed send, her thumb quivering above the little arrow beforehand, it had gone *boom!* Then reverberated for moments after before calming down.

It had taken Ryan almost 24 hours to reply which had been hell for Leah. She thought perhaps she'd typed the wrong thing. Put him off. She'd obsessed over it, checked her phone constantly—even got threatened with it being confiscated in DT at school. But, finally, he had messaged back, not long before her dad had disturbed her. '*I used to walk past you in the mornings. Where did you go? (sad face emoji)'.* OMG! She'd just about died. Don't message back straightaway, play it cool, she'd told herself. Otherwise, she'd seem like a silly little girl, desperate. "Leah?" That was when her dad had walked in.

Over the following weeks, leading up to the May half-term holiday, messages were exchanged at an increasing frequency, sometimes late into the night:

L: *'How old are you?'*

R: *'Fourteen. Where do you live?'*

L: *'Alderleigh. What music do you like?'*

R: *'Singer-songwriters mainly'*

L: *'Me too! Do you like Ed Sheeran?'*

R: *'Love him.'*

L: *'You look like Justin Beiber.'*

R: *'People say that.'*

L: *'Girls?'*

R: *'R u on Snapchat? Add me. Ryan#11'*

L: *'Wots the #11 stand for?'*

R: *'My dad's favourite player. Ryan Giggs. I was named after him. Would u like to watch me play football one day?'*

L: *'Sure.'*

R: *'Send me a picture. Ur so pretty.'* Leah had treasured this one. No boy had ever called her pretty before. 'Fit', maybe, or 'hot'—the stupid, childish boys in her year—but not 'pretty'. It was because Ryan was older, more mature. *I bet he's posh*, she thought. *And rich.*

The ghosts were none too pleased about all this communication. Especially Penny. She didn't like the sound of the boy. He was too pushy. Boys asking for pictures, boys complimenting girls on their looks: they were only usually after one thing…

Chapter Six

The holiday booking request had been accepted, and the day of the family's short break arrived. Elaine was going. Begrudgingly. There was part of Hugh that always knew she would. But the ghosts had been on tenterhooks. Will she? Won't she? It would have defeated the object if she hadn't have gone—backfired spectacularly, like most of their meddling schemes. A pile of luggage, food items and bedding were heaped by the front door. Jake came downstairs with his arms full, baseball cap and headphones on. "How come he gets to take his Xbox?" said Leah. "It's not fair." Jake nodded his head to his music in front of his sister's face, goading her. She hit him.

"Well, why don't you take the Wii or something?" said Hugh.

"Yes, why don't you take the Wii, Leah?" teased Jake.

"Pack it in, Jake," snapped Elaine. "There isn't room for the Wii. You'd have to take all the bits as well. The car's full as it is!"

"I don't want to take the bloody Wii anyway. It's boring. No one plays on Wiis anymore," said Leah.

"Since when?" said Hugh in despair. "You used to love the Wii. That dance game and that." He couldn't believe he was trying to bribe them with technology. That was the whole point of going away: to get away from it.

Watched by the ghosts, items were bundled into the car and strapped to the roof of it, amidst much bickering and griping. Leah sat on the back seat, frantically typing last-minute goodbye messages to Ryan et al. Anyone would have thought she was being taken away to do a stretch in prison, not for a four-day break. The ghosts stood at the window, some of them holding hands, some of them waving, some with their fingers crossed, as the car pulled away. "Well, that's that then," said the colonel. "Well done, men. Mission accomplished."

"And women," said Absinthe.

"Yep, it's in their hands now," said Penny.

Setting off in the car, the children immediately went to put their headphones on. Hugh noticed in the rear-view mirror. "Oh, come on, you two. Don't do that. This is about us spending time together, away from your screens, communicating as a family. I'll put some music on." Leah and Jake groaned and pulled faces. They both knew what he was going to put on. And he did. The standard going-away-on-holiday soundtrack—the best of Crowded House.

The opening bars of *Fall at your Feet* started, and there were more groans from the back seat. Hugh tried to get an impromptu sing-along going, like in the old days. It was embarrassing. "Oh, come on! You used to love this!" The children stared out of their windows, hunkered down in their seats, wishing they were anywhere else.

Elaine did too. All this felt forced, awkward. She was in a foul mood and couldn't shift it. The thought of four days without Facebook, without Wi-Fi, with no release—just the family—seemed like hell. And this made her feel guilty. She snuck onto Facebook one last time, whilst she had 3G, trying to make the most of her last remaining minutes with it. She felt like posting some messages herself. 'Going to hell. See you on the other side.' Hugh glanced across at her, scrolling away. It irked him. There he was, having a go at the kids when she was just as bad. What example did it set?

The journey continued in silence, save for the music. There was no escaping it. It was depressing Jake. Not so much the music itself, but what it represented: the sickly nostalgia of it. He was old enough and savvy enough to know what this holiday was: a last-ditch attempt to keep the family together, to relive the good times. He was all-too-aware this could be the last time that they did this together. He'd heard the conversations, the muffled voices late into the night; his room was across the hall from his parents': 'I just can't do this anymore, Hugh'; 'I can't carry on like this'; 'We're going to have to tell them sooner or later'…

Don't Dream It's Over started playing on the stereo. The song seemed especially poignant. Unexpectedly, a lump appeared in Jake's throat and he stared harder out of the window, sneaking his headphones on to drown out the song.

It didn't take long for the arguing to start. "Mum, Jake's got his headphones on," said Leah.

"Shut up, snitch," said Jake.

"Jake," said Hugh, not unkindly.

"Oh, let him have his headphones on. He doesn't want to listen to this," said Elaine.

"Well, if he's having his headphones on, then so am I," said Leah, plugging her ears. Hugh gave Elaine a look.

Half an hour later, with both Hugh and Elaine preoccupied, they missed the vital turn that they always seemed to miss. Hugh blamed Elaine, for not watching out for it. "Too busy staring at your phone as usual!"

"Well, if you put the address into the satnav like any normal human being, then you wouldn't need me to watch out for it."

"Why do I need the satnav when we've done this journey a dozen times?"

"Er, because, *clearly*, you still don't know the way."

Another 20 minutes and they were at a standstill. They'd hit traffic, heading into Ashbourne. Hugh had wanted to take the scenic route, through the market towns, to see the bunting and that. He always pointed it out to the children—every time. "I knew we should have gone on the bloody M1," muttered Elaine. And then to Hugh, "I told you we should have taken the motorway. This is going to add half an hour to the journey at least."

Hugh had been waiting for this. "Oh, well, you always know best, don't you, Elaine? You can always drive, you know, instead of sitting there on your bloody phone!"

"I didn't want to come in the first place," she said under her breath, staring out of the window. Hugh glared at her then glanced in the rear-view mirror to see if the kids had heard. They had but were pretending that they hadn't.

Chapter Seven

With the family away, it was quiet at Cuckoo House. Too quiet. It had been a novelty at first for the ghosts, having the run of the place, not having to whisper and tiptoe about. They could watch what TV programmes they liked; sleep in what beds they liked; there had been a few arguments over the beds. Being the eldest (in human years), the colonel and Penny got the final say. The youngsters bunked up together. It was like having a sleepover. The pastor preferred the sofa anyway. Leofwine had taken to sleeping in the serving hatch. It was warm in there. Cordingley didn't get a say, as usual.

But before long, boredom set in. The family were a distraction, their own TV show. Without them, the ghosts became more aware of themselves, of what they were, of their own pointless existence. They had too much time to think, got on each other's nerves, and bickered. Sam was like a lovesick puppy dog without Leah. The pastor was nearly as bad without Elaine. Paul made his familiar threats to commit suicide, by revealing himself to the paperboy or the postman. Calypso missed having a man about the place, a real man. A man with blood pulsing through his veins; she missed watching Hugh shower. She prowled the balcony at night, leaning over it, like in the old days, bosom heaving, harassing the male ghosts. "Can I offer you, gentlemen, anything?"

"Thank you, no." This was Cordingley, blushing, twitching and hurrying past.

"What about you, Colonel? Betty told me how you liked it back in the day—what you were doing when you passed away." Calypso made a woofing sound.

"Oh, button your lips, woman."

"These lips probably earned more in a week than you did in a month on your army salary, sugar…"

****

It was the second day without the family, and the twins were goading Paul. "Here's the postman now. He's earlier than normal. Go on, I dare you," said Absinthe.

"I will, you know, don't try me," said Paul.

"You shouldn't joke about such things," said the pastor, looking up from the newspaper—Elaine had forgotten to cancel it.

"I wouldn't worry, Pastor. He's been threatening it for years; he's too miserable to commit suicide," said Penny.

"Hold on, that's not the normal postman. It's a post*lady* by the looks of it," said Juniper.

"A fat postlady!" chuckled Sam.

"And she's on a bike." They watched the portly woman dismount and remove her bag. She plonked it down, out of breath.

"Ugh! Look at those ugly tattoos on her legs. Why do women feel the need to brand themselves in such a way these days? Tattoos are for men, not women. Sailors and the like," said Penny.

"I know. It's ungodly. You see it on the telly all the time," said the pastor. "It would have been unthinkable in my day. No man would go near a woman with tattoos. Except for a harlot, maybe."

At the bottom of the drive, Miss Collins crouched down to unzip her mailbag, whilst craftily checking out the vicinity of Cuckoo House. *This was just like old times*, she thought. What she called a 'recce'. Of course, she had a lot more technology at her disposal these days; that's why the car on the drive wasn't a surprise to her. For the last 24 hours, she'd had a live feed of the house up on one of her many laptops, courtesy of Google Street View. The Berridges must have two cars—most families did—unless there was someone looking after the house for them. The car hadn't moved once, though, in all that time.

Miss Collins pretended to search through the mailbag. It was full of magazines, an oversight on her part. She could have stuffed it full of anything—clothes, scrunched up newspaper, hardly ideal for carting around on a bike. She was out of shape and cursed losing her driving licence. At least she looked the part. Post wasn't the only thing that she'd stolen during her time working for the Royal Mail, before being prosecuted. The uniform had been languishing in her wardrobe ever since, musty and creased. She'd had to iron it. She was no good at ironing. But she enjoyed wearing the uniform; the shorts showed off her calf tattoos.

As for the location of the house, it couldn't be any more perfect. She'd familiarised herself with it on the website. The lane only led up to the property, banked on both sides by high hedges, a large, private garden to the rear. If only it wasn't for that car, it made her nervous.

Little Leah had announced all over social media she was going away with her family for a few days. A recent post, somewhere in the Peak District, checking into some pub or other with the rest of her family, confirmed the fact. Why did people do that? Post where they were constantly, and who they were with. *'I'm not at home, my house is empty, come and rob me!'* Fools. Leah had also happened to mention, during one of their late-night conversations, that she lived in a house that used to be a pub. Cue Google search for pubs in Alderleigh. Only one came up, The Cuckoo Inn. Cue Google search for a postcode for Cuckoo Inn, Alderleigh. The postcode was then programmed into the satnav on Miss Collins's phone. It was all too easy.

She removed her dirty red cap, mopped her brow and scratched her wig, before replacing the cap. After shouldering her bag, she began pushing her bike towards the house, her face flushed from exertion. She kept her eyes peeled for signs of life from within. Getting closer, she searched the façade of the property for an alarm box, peeking out from under the ivy. There didn't appear to be one. People were crafty, though. It could be hidden, or around the side. She would need to do a full check of the perimeter.

Passing the car on the drive, Miss Collins peered inside it. Judging by the paraphernalia scattered about, it appeared to be a woman's. Good. Most likely the mother's. Miss Collins parked the bike by the front door, anticipating the sudden barking of a dog. None came which was a relief. Leah hadn't mentioned a dog. They probably would have taken it with them anyway. Not taking any chances, a fake parcel had been prepared, complete with a stamp and false address on it. She'd made sure it was too big to fit through the letterbox.

Taking a deep breath, Miss Collins pressed the doorbell. Doing this was a risk. The sound echoed throughout the house. She rehearsed in her head what she was going to say: 'Oh, hello. Sorry to disturb you, but could you tell me where this house is (show the parcel)? I'm new to this route, see, and there's no postcode on it...' She waited.

The ghosts, who had jumped at the sound of the doorbell, swarmed about within, some of them peering through the glass in the door. After getting no reply, Miss Collins pressed the doorbell again. And waited again. Still no reply. Satisfied, she made her way around the side of the house with the parcel.

There was no sign of an alarm on that side of the property either. Negotiating a rusty, whining gate, Miss Collins reached the back garden. It was even larger in real life than it had looked on the computer images. A path surrounded the house, widening into a patio to the rear. She followed the path to make sure there wasn't an alarm box on the other side of the house. On the way, she stepped over a white double trapdoor in the ground. A path led away from it, cutting through the lawn to another side gate, buried in the hedge. Through the hedge, she could make out the main road through the village. "Hmm, interesting," she said.

After confirming that there was no alarm fitted to the house, she returned to the trapdoor. It was secured with a chain and padlock. She looked up at the house, then studied the path again to the side gate. It was clear to see that, back in the day, this had been a hatch to the pub's cellar. The dray lorry would have pulled up at the side gate and rolled the barrels down the path to the hatch. This could be a possible way in, a way in without having to cause too much damage. Looking around her, she crouched down to pick up the chain and rattle the padlock. It was locked.

By now, a few of the ghosts that had tracked the woman's progress to the rear of the property had begun to take an even keener interest. They were watching out of the kitchen window. There was nothing that unusual about a post lady delivering a parcel around the back of the house—even though she was a new one—but checking padlocks? "What on earth's she doing?" said Absinthe. "You lot, come and look at this!" The pastor and Paul joined them.

"Perhaps she's just checking to see if she can put the parcel down there, to keep it safe," said Penny.

"I don't like the look of her," said Juniper.

"Neither do I," said Sam.

"You're both being ridiculous as usual," said Cordingley. "Bored, I expect."

"Wait, what's she doing now? She's coming to the window!" said the pastor.

As the ghosts looked on, to their horror, Miss Collins came and pressed her face against the kitchen window. They recoiled in fright, taking a few steps back. The pastor made the sign of the cross. The woman had her hands cupped over her small, mean eyes to see better. The peak of her cap was pushed flat against the window, her pudgy, squashed hands yellow against the glass, her teeth stained brown. "Ugh! Make her go away, someone!" said Penny.

Absinthe walked up to the window and breathed hard, straight into the woman's face. The window clouded over, cold not hot, obscuring the interloper's view. Miss Collins tried to wipe the mist away with her sleeve but couldn't. A puzzled look came over her face, and she backed off, adjusting her cap. With one last look at the trapdoor, then at the house and all around, still clutching her parcel, she walked back around the side of the house. "Where's she going?" said Juniper.

The ghosts heard the gate go again. They all moved to the front of the house, in a flock as one, where the woman reappeared. As they watched, she put the parcel back in the bag, got on her bike and pedalled away.

"She's going away," said Absinthe. Feeling braver, Sam banged on the window and pulled a face, but the woman didn't turn around. Probably didn't hear over the gravel.

"Someone wake the colonel up, I think he ought to know," said Penny.

"Know what? A postlady tried to deliver a parcel?" said Cordingley.

"But she didn't deliver it, though, did she? She took it away with her," said Absinthe.

"And your point being?"

"Oh, shut up, Cordingley."

Chapter Eight

By the end of that day, the suspicious postlady was all but forgotten about, and boredom had returned. There was nothing to do but go to bed. Most of the ghosts had already turned in for the night. Calypso was up and about, as usual, treading the boards, trying to pedal her wares to no one in particular. The twins were downstairs, putting some finishing touches to some scented candles they had made for Elaine; the same colour as some she had, but more therapeutic.

It was just approaching the witching hour when a noise disturbed them: the distinct whine of the side gate opening. It was left to bang in the wind for a few moments then was firmly squeaked closed. The twins looked at each other wide-eyed. Even ghosts get scared of bumps in the night. "Is everyone inside?" whispered Juniper.

"Yes, I think so." They both got up and scuttled to the landing.

"Calypso! Are you upstairs?" called Juniper.

"I sure am, sugar. Have you found me a man?" She floated down the stairs.

"Did you just hear the gate opening and closing?"

"No, why?"

"Well, it did," said Absinthe.

"Maybe my prayers have been answered," said Calypso.

There was a creak on the landing above, making the twins jump. Penny appeared, yawning, rubbing her hair. She could never sleep properly till all the younger ghosts were in bed. "Did I just hear the gate go, or was I dreaming?" she said.

"No, we heard it too," said Juniper.

"Thought so. That's strange. Is everyone here?" Penny shuffled down the stairs to join them.

"Yes, we think so," said Absinthe.

Just then, there was the rattling of a chain from out the back of the house. Penny froze, halfway down the stairs. The twins grabbed hold of each other. Having not been around to witness today's unwanted visitor, Calypso let out a deep villainous chuckle. "Maybe it's Jacob Marley! Moohaahaahaa!" She tickled the girls in the ribs.

"Pack it in, Calypso!" said Penny. "This isn't funny. It's the same sound from today, the chain on the cellar hatch. Listen!" The chain clinked, banging against the hatch as if being moved about.

"Come on, let's go and investigate," said Calypso.

"No, I'm scared," said Juniper.

"Me too," said Absinthe.

"Well, I'm not," said Calypso. "Come on, Penny." She took her elbow.

"The kitchen window," said Penny. And they headed off. The twins looked at each other, then followed them, still clutching onto each other.

By the time they'd reached the kitchen, Calypso and Penny were already at the window. Penny gasped and put her hand to her mouth. "It's her!" she said, making the hair on the twins' arms and necks stand on end.

"Who?" said Calypso.

"The postwoman from today. She's come back!"

"Post*woman*? Looks more like a man to me. Or a rug muncher. And trust me, I've known a few of them in my time," said Calypso.

"What do you mean, a rug munch—actually, I don't want to know," said Penny.

The twins came to join them at the window, cautiously peering around Penny, as if they could be seen. Outside, silhouetted against the purple night, a portly figure was squatting down at the cellar hatch, rooting around in some sort of rucksack. The shape of the person was unmistakeable and so was that peaked cap. "Oh my God. It *is* her!" said Juniper.

"But where's her hair gone?" said Absinthe.

"Maybe it's tucked into her cap," said Penny.

"What's she doing?" said Absinthe.

"She's trying to get in," said Calypso.

"Don't say that. Don't say those words!" said Juniper.

The woman pulled some sort of metal cutters from out of her rucksack. She appeared to be wearing gloves. The ghosts watched in disbelief as she picked up the chain, placed it between the cutters and began to squeeze. "Cheeky bitch!" said Calypso. But the chain wouldn't give. They heard the woman mutter something between clenched teeth. She squeezed again, harder, her meaty arms quivering with the effort. Suddenly. the cutters bit through the chain, surprising her, and she fell backwards onto her arse and swore.

The ghosts gasped. "She's trying to get in!" said Juniper.

"I told you she was trying to get in!" said Calypso.

"But why? What does she want from us? Girls, wake the colonel, quick! And the pastor. And Sam. Wake them all!" cried Penny.

The twins scurried off, glad to be going upstairs.

As quietly as possible, Miss Collins freed the chain from the handles of the double doors. It slithered, snake-like, from its shackle. She threw it on the grass. An owl hooted, startling her. After a quick look around, she pulled open the first trapdoor. It creaked loudly as she folded it back. She winced, looking over her shoulder again. In stark contrast to the warm night air, a cold draft wafted up from the cellar below. It smelt musty, damp and old, like a dungeon in a castle. She folded back the second door.

Miss Collins reached into her rucksack again and pulled out a torch. She shone the torch into the hatch. What met her was a reflective, criss-crossed net of cobwebs, barring the way in. She pulled a face and began ripping them apart. They clung to her gloves, sticky as glue, and she had to keep wiping them on her jacket.

Once the majority of the cobwebs had been cleared, she could see down into the cellar better. Her torch lit up a set of steep, narrow, wooden steps. They were curved in the middle, well worn, and framed on each side by a metal rail, or pair of runners. She followed the rails downwards with her torch. At the bottom of the steps, on the cellar floor, was an old hessian sack or cushion. The whole thing clearly formed a kind of chute for the barrels. It was amazing that it was all still left like this.

Leaving her rucksack behind, Miss Collins tentatively made her way down into the cellar, brushing aside more cobwebs as she went. She pulled the hatch doors to behind her. Using the torch as a guide, she negotiated her considerable bulk down the precarious stairs; twice, nearly losing her footing. Not being able to see further than the torch beam was quite unnerving. There was no doubt about it: it was creepy down there.

Once at the bottom, she stepped onto the hessian cushion. It was split at the seams and let out a puff of dust and stuffing. The tiny flecks shimmered in the light of the torch as she waved it about the cellar. Junk and the odd metal barrel were lit up, dusty corners and more cobwebs. A flicker of movement and a scurrying sound startled her. She jerked her torch in its direction, but too late. A rat? She shuddered and carried on shining the torch. It alighted on another set of steps opposite, made of stone this time. And at the top of them, just what she was looking for. A door. A way out—or way in, depending on which way you looked at it.

She made straight for the steps, not wanting to spend any more time in that cellar than necessary. Her foot hit an old jar on the way, sending it rolling and clattering into a dark corner. Cue more scratching and scurrying. She speeded up, a hint of panic creeping in; she'd read too many James Herbert books about giant rats when she was younger. Mounting the first step, she kept her eyes and the torch beam firmly trained on the door above. If it was locked it would be game over unless she could force her way in somehow. She reached the door, placed a gloved hand on the inner latch and lifted the bar. It gave straight away, and she pulled the door towards her, praying it wasn't locked. To her immense relief, it creaked open, prompting a surge of adrenaline to course through her. She was in.

By now, most of the ghosts had congregated in the lounge, huddled together. They felt the same emotions that any living person would, having an intruder force their way into your home in the dead of night: fear, anger and indignation. Rooted to the spot, they watched the cellar door swing inwards. Yellow torchlight spilt into the lounge. The light was quickly extinguished, and a large, shadowy figure emerged. The woman was breathing heavily. The sound was loud, intrusive. She pulled the door closed behind her and scanned the room. She looked right at them, right through them; it was most unnerving. Sam hid behind Penny.

Once her eyes had adjusted to the light, Miss Collins made a beeline for the front window of the lounge. The ghosts parted into two groups. As she pulled the curtains to, she heard a hissing sound behind her and snapped her head around. With the curtains drawn, she dared to click on the torch but kept a gloved hand over the beam. She searched the room for the source of the noise—a cat somewhere, she'd heard it distinctly, a pair of eyes reflecting back at her in the dark—but saw nothing. She shrugged and gave up. *Why was it so damn cold in here?* she thought.

Guided by the torch, she made her way out of the room and into a large hallway. She shone the torch up the stairs. Above was a galleried landing. A smile crept across her face. Upstairs would be what she had come for: the girl's room. A window into her life. More information, more ammunition. She would soak it up, bag herself a trophy, maybe.

But first, where was the bathroom? She needed a shit. This always happened when she was on a job—the excitement, the adrenaline, the fear. Sometimes she couldn't wait and had to go in a garden, in some bushes, behind a bin. It was almost like her calling card. She made her way upstairs.

The ghosts shuffled out of the lounge and gathered at the bottom of the stairs. "Where's she going?" whispered Penny.

"I don't know, but she gives me the creeps," said Juniper.

"There's the devil in her," said the pastor, "he of the cloven hoof. She reeks of him."

"We must stop this intruder. It's an outrage, forcing her way in here!" said the colonel.

"But how?" said Penny.

"Scare her," said Absinthe. "We're ghosts, aren't we?"

They watched as Miss Collins pushed different doors open on the landing, peering into rooms. "She's going into the bathroom!" said Penny. "Come on."

The ghosts crept up the stairs in a slow-moving mist. The bathroom door had been left ajar and was framed by yellow torchlight. They gathered outside it, listening. There was the sudden, nausea-inducing sound of bowels being emptied, loudly and violently, accompanied by a groan, from within. The ghosts looked at each other in disgust, screwing up their faces. An equally repugnant stench drifted out from under the bathroom door and onto the hallway. It was worse for those closest to it. Some of the ghosts moved away, covering their noses, some gagging silently.

The toilet was flushed and there was the rustling of clothes. They waited for the sound of the sink tap being turned on. It didn't happen. Instead, the bathroom door opened. *Dirty bitch*, they all thought, pressing themselves against the walls on either side of the door. The woman walked past them, putting her gloves back on. Being the most demonstrative of the ghosts, Absinthe showed her displeasure by breathing on the intruder hard. Miss Collins shivered in response, rubbing her neck.

They watched as she briefly shone a torch into a room, one of the spare rooms. Seemingly uninterested, she pulled the door to again. Then she turned and tried the door opposite, peering in and waving her torch about; this time for longer, much longer. That twisted smile reappeared, and after a quick glance down the corridor, she headed into the room. The ghosts looked at each other. "She's going into Leah's room!" said the colonel.

He marched off, gesturing with his cane for them to follow. Unable to help himself, Sam let out a strange, muffled cry and tugged at Juniper's sleeve. "Wait!" she whispered. "Sam's got something to say."

The colonel stopped. "Well, what is it, boy? Spit it out!"

They all turned to Sam. Unused to such scrutiny, he blushed and looked down, adopting a stammer. "What is it, Sam? It's okay. Speak up," said Penny.

"The cap," he finally managed, "I recognise the cap."

"What cap?" said the colonel.

"The one she's wearing. It's the same as Ryan's," said Sam.

"Who's Ryan?" said Calypso.

"The boy, the one she's been talking to on the computer," said Sam.

"I think he's right, you know," said Penny.

"The boy she's been talking to on the computer? Why wasn't I informed of this?" said Cordingley, thrusting his puny grey chest out.

"Keep your voice down, Cordingley," hissed Penny. "Leah's not your department, that's why."

"No, but computers are."

"Cordingley's right, he should have been informed," said the colonel.

"Well, the cap's probably just a coincidence anyway," said Penny.

"I doubt it," said Cordingley. "I really should have been privy to this information earlier. That's the same woman that tried to get in this morning. If I'd known this, I would have attached more significance to it. The fiend's obviously got an unhealthy obsession with the girl. She's gone straight to her room!"

"But Leah's been talking to a young boy, the same age as her, not a big fat woman!" said Penny.

Cordingley pushed his glasses up on his nose and gave her a withering look. "Technology, dear woman, technology. Have you never heard of Photoshop?"

"Don't 'dear woman' me, you pompous prat, or I'll photo shop you!" said Penny, feeling somehow responsible that she'd let this happen.

"Will you two shut up! We haven't got time for this. That beast could be doing anything in there right now, laying her grubby hands on everything," said Absinthe. As if to emphasise the fact, they heard the curtains being drawn in Leah's room. "Come on!" she said, setting off.

"Thank God she's got gloves on, is all I can say," said the pastor, following her.

As the ghosts shuffled into the bedroom, Miss Collins was shining her torch into Leah's wardrobe. She suddenly felt the temperature plummet and shuddered again. *Why was it so bloody cold in this house?* She ran her fingers over the clothes hanging up. The coat hangers click-clacked under her gloves.

To the ghosts' astonishment and repulsion, she then leant forward to sniff the clothes, burying her face in them.

When she'd drunk her fill, she withdrew her head from the wardrobe and shone her torch around the room. It settled on the posters on the walls, hovering over them. Shawn Mendes. Jamie Lawson—more singer-songwriters. *Log it*, she thought. A small bookshelf, mainly filled with Harry Potter books. *Log it*. Moving on, she spotted an acoustic guitar in a case, propped in a corner. *Log it*. There were clothes strewn about, and a chest of drawers topped with bric-à-brac, trinkets and a smiley face money jar. The torch beam swung to Leah's bed, and Miss Collins made straight for it. After sniffing the pillow first, she lay down with her hands behind her head, a satisfied smile on her face.

After a few moments, she became restless again. She wanted a memento, a trophy to take with her. It was another of her habits. The torch searched the room again and returned to the chest of drawers, to the bric-à-brac on top. Seeing nothing of fancy, she lowered the beam to the drawers themselves, some of which were open. Her face twitched, and she suddenly got up.

As she walked towards the chest, Penny gestured frantically to the other ghosts, mouthing something they didn't understand. "What?" they mouthed back.

"Do something! Somebody do something!" she mouthed again.

Miss Collins pulled open the top drawer and shone in her torch. As she began to rummage about, she was distracted by something off to her right: a glimmer of light in the darkness. She turned her head. The light was getting stronger. It was tall, man-shaped. Before her eyes, against the wall, as if lit up

80

by a projector, a shimmering apparition appeared. It was a man in a suit, looking grim and sad. His hollow eyes were staring right at her. The skin over Miss Collins's entire body crawled and shrank and pimpled. "What the *fuck!*" she said.

Just then, there was an icy blast and a voice from behind, hissing in her left ear: "*GET... OUT!*" The drawer slammed shut, trapping her hands. Even with gloves on it hurt and she let out a shriek. "*Jesus Christ!*" She looked again to the right, but the apparition had gone.

Miss Collins fled from the house, back the way she'd come, through the cellar and out of the hatch. All but two of the ghosts followed her in a swarm, willing her away, stronger and braver now. She slammed the doors of the hatch behind her as if she could trap whatever she had witnessed within. Without even bothering to replace the chain, she stuffed her tools back in her bag and ran to her bike. She wobbled down the drive on it, looking over her shoulder at the imposing silhouetted house, vowing never to return.

Meanwhile, inside, the ghosts were charging back upstairs. They reached Leah's room and burst in. Absinthe was sitting slumped against the wall. She looked spent; a pale imitation of herself; dimmer, less defined, guttering like an oil lamp about to burn out. "*Absinthe!*" screamed Juniper. But Absinthe didn't look up, and Juniper ran to her twin. "Absinthe, look at me," she said, brushing some of her sister's hair aside. Absinthe's head lolled and struggled to support itself. The ghosts gathered around, distraught. "Don't you leave me, Absinthe! Look at me!" Absinthe tried to focus on her sister, tried to speak. "Don't speak, just rest. It's OK," said Juniper. But Absinthe tried again. "What is it? Whisper to me," Juniper said, leaning in. Absinthe managed to whisper

81

something in her ear, then they pressed their heads together, as if in prayer.

"What is it? What did she say?" said Penny, crouching down. She put her hand on Juniper's shoulder and stroked Absinthe's hair.

"Paul's gone. She said, 'Paul's gone.'" The ghosts drew a collective intake of breath. In all the commotion, they'd forgotten about Paul. He was nowhere to be seen. There were a few sniffles.

"I never thought he'd do it," said the pastor.

"He was a good man," said the colonel, "braver than we gave him credit for."

"Went out in style," added Calypso.

"He'll be with his beloved now. It's what he always wanted," said the pastor. "Let us pray for him."

****

Once safely back home, Miss Collins wheeled her bike inside, threw her bag down, and locked the door behind her, putting the latch on for good measure. She was still in shock, still traumatised, and struggling to comprehend what had just happened. Voices in her head, she was used to those; that's what she took the tablets for, or was supposed to. But ghostly apparitions, drawers slamming shut? Was she really losing her marbles? Or had she just got spooked? A combination of that creepy cellar and that cat that had never materialised. Perhaps she was getting too old for this shit. She knew one thing; she had lost all interest in that girl now. She was bad juju. It had scared her off. Move on.

After hiding her gear, she grabbed a can of cider from the fridge and opened a bag of tortilla chips. Fistfuls of them were stuffed into her mouth. She gorged on them, washing them down with the cider. It was a comfort. She rolled a fag with shaky hands and switched on a laptop. Going straight to Ryan's profile, she went to the 'friends' section. There weren't many. She clicked on Leah's face. Shame, she'd put in a lot of graft on this one. And she was a stunner, too. Miss Collins toyed with going through their messages together, looking at the pictures Leah had sent; one last reminisce. But, no. Think about what had happened at that house. She shuddered and clicked the little blue man with the tick by him. Three options came up. A fat cheesy orange finger hovered over the unfriend button. She pressed it before she could change her mind. Done.

Chapter Nine

The Berridges' break had started badly and gone downhill from there. On arrival, Hugh had twinged his back, hoisting the large suitcase down from the roof of the car. Jake had had to carry it up the steep steps to the cottage. This had put Hugh in a foul mood from the outset, as pretty much all of his planned activities involved walking or climbing. He couldn't even drive.

For decency's sake, they all tried to go through the motions, pretending everything was normal. But everything had lost its magic. Bakewell town was heaving and there was nowhere to park; the last thing the kids wanted to do was traipse around the shops with no intention of buying anything, or eating cake anyway. Dovedale was just painful: nothing but steps. Climbing Thorpe Cloud was out of the question. They didn't get the traditional photo of them all on the stepping stones taken (normally by a foreigner) for possibly the first time ever. They had a photo board at home with the same shot throughout the years, to see how they'd all grown and changed: the kids from toddlers to adolescents, the adults widening and greying. Funnily enough, the photo board hadn't been seen since the move. The climb to the cable cars at The Heights of Abraham was, again, out of the question.

And the usual visit to Monsal Head, to see the stunning view and watch the sun go down, was cancelled due to an unseasonal downpour. To top it all off, the local pub near the cottage had changed hands and was no longer an Indian restaurant. It was now a 'buy one get one free'. This was probably more galling than anything else, especially for Elaine. It was the only thing she had been looking forward to. The disappointment made her want to cry.

The only respite had been a visit to Matlock Bath. Purely because there was a café-style chip shop there with free Wi-Fi. It was a relief for all of them, though the adults wouldn't admit it: a little oasis amongst the mountains and hills. An opportunity to temporarily reconnect with the rest of the world, to relieve the boredom. Spirits were briefly lifted, frayed tempers were assuaged. A comfortable silence descended, like when a family were all tucking into a decent meal together. Hugh caught up with the sports news and checked his e-mails. Elaine went on Facebook. Jake checked out what his mates had been up to. Leah went on anything and everything she could in a bit of social media frenzy: posting, liking and checking in.

Ryan had sent a new message a day or so ago. This was what she'd been hoping for. It gave her a thrill, but also made her mad. What if he thought she didn't care because she hadn't replied within 24 hours? The message said: '*Miss u. Wen r u back? Send another pic. x.*' Leah looked around her. The family were all busy on their phones, even Dad. Hypocrite. She tidied her hair, straightened it, and checked her image in the phone camera. Why hadn't she put some makeup on, Goddamnit? Oh well, it would have to do. She sucked in her cheeks and tried to look sophisticated and grown-up. Click. It was done. She wrote: '*Sorry. No bloody wifi. Miss u 2. Back Tues. x.*' Send.

Hugh was the first to tire of looking at his phone, and it didn't take long for the bickering to start back up. An argument ensued over the fact that Leah didn't want any chips. It was hard to get her to eat at the best of times. "How can you not want any chips? That was the whole reason for us coming here. We always get chips," said Hugh.

"I just don't want any. They're fattening," said Leah.

"You need fattening up. You're too thin," said Hugh.

"Hugh. I've told you not to say that to her," said Elaine.

"I'll have a bottle of water instead," said Leah.

"I'm not paying two quid for a bottle of water, just because it says, 'local bloody spring water' on it!" said Hugh.

"Let her have her water. It's no more than the chips would cost," said Elaine.

"No, it's the principle of the thing! You can have some tap water instead." Hugh got up. "Anyone else wants a drink? A can of pop?" Elaine glared at him.

"I'll have a Tango," said Jake.

"Oh, so he can have a can of fizzy drink, but I can't have water! That's so hypocritical," Leah said, slumping down in her seat.

Hugh ignored her. "Elaine? Drink?"

"No."

"You sure you don't want any chips, Leah?"

"No, I don't want any bloody chips!"

Leah got her bottle of water after all, and the chips were eaten in strained silence. They were soggy. Elaine threw half of hers away. This irked Hugh. He'd enjoyed his chips, and his back was feeling slightly better. He'd taken three

Ibuprofen. Once they'd all finished, he said, "Right, who wants to go to the amusement arcades?" There were groans all around.

"Do we have to?" said Leah.

"Can't we just go back to the cottage?" said Jake.

"And do what?" said Hugh.

"He just wants to go on his Xbox," said Leah.

"Shut up, Leah!" said Jake. Hugh looked at Elaine for support. None came. She wouldn't have minded going back to the cottage herself; she could do with sleep.

****

Homeward bound, break over, Elaine could honestly say she felt worse than before they went. Seeing Cuckoo House again, as they turned into the drive, confirmed it. There wasn't a scrap of the feeling of being glad to be home: no warmth, no fondness for the property. It reminded her of everything that was wrong; they'd just put their problems on hold for a few days. Her so-called 'marriage' had become an exercise in sadomasochism—like pouring hot water on a burn. And now she'd got three suitcases of dirty washing to deal with. What had been the point in it all?

Unlike her mother, Leah couldn't wait to get back home. She had been on tenterhooks for the last part of the journey. The minute she'd got 3G again, she'd logged onto Facebook. Notifications kept popping up, messages, loads of them. This cheered her up; it was her equivalent of gumballs raining out of a gumball machine. She couldn't wait to see what Ryan had messaged in response to the picture she had sent him yesterday.

But, of all the messages, there didn't seem to be any from Ryan. Perhaps he hadn't received the picture. It had definitely been sent. She posted a new public message, hoping to prompt him: '*Back in the real world. Five minutes from Wifi! (double smiley face)*', though she didn't feel smiley. The holiday had been a disaster, what with Dad's back, Jake not speaking, and Mum and Dad rowing all the time. Leah kept her phone in her lap, checking it obsessively, every ten seconds or so. The battery was getting dangerously low.

As the family pulled up on the drive, Sam rushed to the window. "They're back, they're back!" he cried, bouncing up and down, thrilled to see Leah again, someone his own age. The other ghosts that were downstairs shot up from their respective resting places to join him.

"They're back!" called Penny up the stairs, before joining the rest of the group at the window.

The family's faces were scrutinised as they got out of the car, for signs of happiness, to see if the break had been reparative, had brought them back together. Elaine had been driving, which was unusual. She didn't look any happier. Leah was glued to her phone, as usual, looking anxious. Jake was struggling to get the large suitcase down from the roof of the car on his own. As for Hugh, he seemed to be taking an age to get out of the car. He looked in pain.

Penny was the first to acknowledge what all the ghosts were thinking; "They don't look any happier. They look even more miserable."

"They do. How is that possible?" said Juniper.

"What's wrong with Hugh? He can barely walk," said Absinthe.

"He's holding his back," said Penny.

"This is not good. Not good at all," said the pastor. "It didn't work. Our plan didn't work."

"No. Looks like it backfired, as usual—like all our plans," said Penny. "The colonel won't be pleased."

"It was a foolish idea anyway," said Cordingley. Penny was just about to give him the sharp end of her tongue when there was the sound of keys in the door.

"Quick. Everyone make way. They're coming in!" said Juniper.

The suitcases were dumped by the front door and Leah ran straight upstairs. Jake began rummaging around in the luggage for his Xbox. Elaine looked haggard, practically suicidal. She shivered and put a hand on the radiator in the hallway. "Hugh, did you turn the heating off before we went away?" Her tone was curt.

"Yes, why?"

"Bloody typical. You could have left it on low. It's freezing in here! God, I hate this house."

"Well, what's the point in having the heating on if we're not here?"

Jake tried to slink upstairs with his Xbox; he could feel another argument brewing. "Er, can somebody put these suitcases out the back before you all disappear? I'll deal with them later," said Elaine. Jake reversed his steps.

"Why? Where are you going?" said Hugh, watching Elaine climb the stairs.

"Bed."

Once in his room, Jake plugged everything back in. It was good to be back. He was looking forward to getting back online with his mates: to feel that sense of company and comradeship. An escape from the real world. So why did he feel so sad then? It felt as if the stuffing had been knocked out of him. As if the 'child' had been knocked out of him like when you discover there's no Santa Claus. He didn't have his usual cockiness and bravado when he rejoined the game. There wasn't the usual cry of "*Whaaatsuuup!*" He just slipped back online quietly.

Down the hallway, Leah was refreshing her Facebook messages on her tablet. Her phone had died. It was charging. She'd had three new likes for the picture she'd sent, a couple of comments, welcoming her back. None from Ryan. Perhaps he wasn't online. She decided to send him a private message, letting him know she was back. She wanted to meet up with him, perhaps watch him play football; she felt ready for it now.

Opening up Facebook messenger, she expected to see the message feed between them right at the top, along with his picture; it usually was of late. She spoke to him more than anyone and liked to keep their conversations rather than delete them, so she could go through them later. But his picture wasn't there. That was funny. She scrolled down, further and further. There was everyone but him. She used the search icon and typed in his name, but it didn't come up. A little pang of doubt pricked at her.

Trying to ignore the rising panic she felt, she went to her profile and clicked on friends. Again, she typed his name into the search bar. 'R-Y'… nothing. 'A-N'… still nothing. What the hell? With trembling fingers, she typed in his whole name. It didn't come up. Struggling to comprehend what was happening, she scrolled through all of her friends alphabetically. It took an age, and with each flick of the thumb, it was as if a bell tolled as the insignificant faces went skidding past; people that meant nothing to her. She reached the *R*s. Rachaels, Rebeccas, Roberts... Why did the second letter have to be a Y? She was now into the *S*s. Still no Ryan. She scrolled back, hoping she'd missed him somehow. She hadn't. She had to face facts: he'd unfriended her. She'd never been unfriended before, by anyone. Ever.

It was like a poison dart, swiftly piercing her heart, its toxin spreading to the rest of her body. Tears welled up in her eyes. A lump appeared in her throat. She felt her whole world come tumbling down around her. Typing his name into the general search bar, his profile came up, his picture, his face that had meant so much to her. *So he was still on Facebook then.* This made it worse, cruel somehow. *Should she send him a message? Ask him why? Was she too fat? Too spotty? Not pretty enough? But that would seem desperate. She was desperate. She wanted to know why.*

Unable to bring herself to do it, Leah threw the tablet on the floor and went to lie down. As she did so the device buzzed, as if in response to its treatment. A notification had come through, and a bolt of hope shot through her. She grabbed the tablet, wiping her eyes and spinning onto her back. It was a Facebook notification. She prodded the orange circle desperately, still hoping, her heart thumping. '*Lucy O'Brien liked your post.*' "Aagh!" Tossing the tablet back onto the floor, Leah crawled under the bedcover—to go to sleep, to blot it all out: just like her mother. Curling into a ball, she wept quietly into her pillow; the pillow that unbeknownst to her, only yesterday, had been occupied by her Ryan.

Leah was woken sometime later by raised voices downstairs: nothing new there. Would it never end? Then the Ryan thing came back to her. It hurt all over again. She had nothing in her life now, nothing to get up for. She covered her head with her pillow. There was the sound of footsteps coming up the stairs, retreating down the landing. She heard a muffled conversation between her dad and Jake. Then the sound of a door closing, her dad's footsteps getting closer, louder, till they were outside her door. There was a knock on the door. "Leah, can I come in?" Without waiting for a reply, he burst in. "Is everything—" He stopped. "Why are you in bed?" He sounded annoyed. "Never mind. Has anything been moved in here—or taken?"

Leah popped her head out from under the cover. She'd been expecting a lecture: something about how lazy she and her brother were, how they needed to do more around the house to help Mum. "Taken? No, why?" She sat up.

"Someone's been in the house while we were away. An intruder."

"An intruder? How do you know?" Leah pulled her bedcover up to her neck at the thought, her eyes scanning the room.

"The padlock chain to the cellar's been cut."

"Ugh. That's horrible," she shuddered. "Wasn't the cellar door locked?"

"No, I had to go in there last minute before we went away. Must have forgotten to lock it."

"Well, what have they taken? Not Grandma's jewellery?"

"No, that's the first thing we checked. Nothing seems to be missing at all so far, nothing expensive anyway, which is odd. But I haven't checked everywhere yet."

"Maybe they got disturbed. Or maybe they got disturbed trying to get in."

"No, they definitely got in. The lounge curtains were closed. We always leave the front curtains open when we go away. It looks suspicious otherwise. Were *these* curtains closed when you came back?" Hugh walked over to the window.

"Yes, I think so. I haven't touched them."

"You think so? Well, were they or weren't they? It's important, Leah. Think!" He snatched the curtains open to see the room better, then winced and clutched the base of his back.

"I said, I think so!"

"Well, is anything missing? Look!" He cast his arm around the room, which was a bit of a shambles.

"I don't know. Not that I can see. I've just woken up!"

"I'm surprised you can see anything in here. It's a tip. Let me know if you notice anything. And have a tidy up, please!" With that, he hobbled quickly out.

Leah could hear her dad stomping around the house, opening and closing doors. Then him and her mum arguing again. "Well, if someone hadn't had left the cellar door unlocked, this wouldn't have happened!" said Elaine.

"Oh, there we go. It's my fault as usual. My fault that we got broken into! Course it is."

"I'm sorry, but that cellar door really should have been checked. What's to stop them from coming back now? Perhaps that was the plan. Perhaps they were just casing the joint. You're going to have to tell the police."

"Tell them what? Nothing's been taken."

"Attempted break-in."

"It wasn't attempted, they did break-in."

"Well, break-in then! It needs to be logged, in case they come back!"

"Stop saying that, Elaine. You'll scare the children."

"I'm just being realistic"—and then in a lower voice—"and that decides it, I don't want to stay here any longer. We're putting the house up for sale. I've never liked the place."

"Oh, any excuse, isn't it? Any excuse just to give in... That's right! Run away as usual!"

"Phone the police!"

"You phone them. I'm going to the hardware shop to get a new chain, something useful!"

"I thought you couldn't drive!"

A door slammed.

Chapter Ten

The police *were* informed of the break-in. They paid a routine visit to Cuckoo House, took some details, dusted for prints. The officers were of the impression that the intruder or intruders were probably disturbed, rather than it being a casing job. Once these people were in, they took their chance, rarely running the risk of coming back.

The Berridges felt a little uneasy in their beds at night, and all slept with some sort of weapon close by. Due to his back playing up, Hugh felt particularly vulnerable and useless in view to protecting his family. It was bad timing. He had taken to doing what he called a security check before turning in for the night, shuffling around the house in his slippers and dressing gown, checking all the windows and doors. A padlock had been placed on the cellar door into the lounge. The idea of getting an exterior security light set up was mooted by him. "What's the point if we're selling up?" was Elaine's response. *Talk about shutting the stable door after the horse has bolted*, she thought.

The ghosts did their best to help but were feeling deflated and unsettled themselves; what with the disappointment of the break going awry, the break-in and, worst of all, losing one of their own. They hadn't lost anyone since 'The Time of Great

Unrest', which was how they referred to the time of upheaval when the house was being renovated. A period of reflection and mourning ensued. They were careful not to make too much noise, especially at night, so as not to scare the family unnecessarily. The only positive was that that 'thing' had stopped contacting Leah—even though she was clearly distraught about it. But she was young; she'd get over it. Good riddance to bad rubbish. At least Paul's passing hadn't been in vain.

Absinthe was soon back to her normal self—she was strong—and she helped her sister in trying to ease Hugh's back pain. The only position he could sleep in to be comfortable was on his side. This was ideal, as it gave them easy access to the problem area. Absinthe gently lifted the bed cover up on Hugh's side of the bed, whilst Juniper placed her hands a centimetre or so from the base of his back. She let them hover in a circle whilst concentrating, an ancient natural healing technique similar to Reiki. Instead of generating heat, however, Absinthe generated a numbing sensation that lasted, comparable to having a bag of frozen peas held against your back—without the burn.

In the morning, Hugh found he wasn't so stiff. He could move without being in pain. So, in turn, became more mobile throughout the day, thus gradually repairing his back. After a few nights of this, he was almost back to normal. He put it down to Ibuprofen and lager, which he'd got in the habit of consuming together from about 11 a.m. since being off work. He was putting on more weight around his middle. It made him hate himself.

Leah just wanted the half-term to end. She used to look forward to the school holidays, hanging around in the park with her friends. But now she dreaded them. Being stuck out there, people had stopped bothering with her, seemed to have forgotten about her. She was no longer part of the in-crowd. This made her feel isolated and left out. Seeing all their posts on Facebook made it worse. Why wasn't she invited to their impromptu get-togethers?

But then going back to school raised the prospect of having to confess about Ryan unfriending her. Leah felt foolish, embarrassed. What would she say when her so-called friends asked her about him? It had made her popular for a while, interesting. She had never felt so low, so alone. She was barely eating. Her parents were always rowing or not speaking. Jake never spoke to her. Sometimes she noticed him looking at her, picking at her dinner. She wanted to scream at him.

For the first time, she considered harming herself. Really doing it. She'd thought about it before. A girl at school did it. She had a brother that died, and his memorial page on Facebook got trolled. Leah spied her metal house pin from school on top of her chest of drawers. As Penny and Sam looked on, horrified, she picked it up, then rolled up the sleeve of her jumper. She drew the sharp point of the pin across the back of her forearm. Experimenting. Harder each time, increasing the pressure. The pin left white lines in its wake. But she couldn't pluck up the courage to pierce the skin. She pressed the point into her thumb instead, to test the sharpness of it, to feel the pain. The soft flesh there punctured easily, surprising her. A crimson bubble appeared and wouldn't stop getting bigger. It hurt. Leah panicked and sucked her thumb. The blood tasted gross, metallic. Seeing it like that—on the outside instead of the inside—put her off. She couldn't do that, could she? She ran to the bathroom to get a tissue. Penny hid the metal badge and anything else sharp in Leah's room too. These were worrying times. The ghosts took turns watching over the girl.

Come Monday morning, Jake was happy returning to school. He was sick of the atmosphere at home, sick of the silence during the day, sick of the arguing at night. He listened to music to drown his parents out till he fell to sleep. *Didn't Leah hear them too? Did she know? Should he tell her?* They barely saw each other at home—him and Leah—only at the dinner table. She was looking pale and thin. He wanted to talk to her about it. Sometimes he wished his parents would just get it over and done with. There was a feeling of impending doom, of waiting for the axe to fall.

Out of habit, Leah watched out for Ryan from the school bus, the last bit up the hill where the two centipedes of children from both schools snaked past each other in opposite directions; the burgundy of the academy, the grey of King's. Her stomach churned, thinking about him. She'd never managed to spot him before—too many kids, too many faces—it would be ironic if she did now. It didn't help that she'd never seen his hair properly, to know what it looked like. She'd always imagined he had a quiff, combed neatly back.

****

They say 'be careful what you wish for'… Later that same day, after a frozen pizza dinner particularly pregnant with silence, Jake and his sister were politely asked not to go back upstairs, but to go into the lounge for 'a chat'. Jake's stomach dropped, and the colour left his face. He knew what this was about—and now that the time had come, he felt sick. His younger sister, in comparison—blissfully unaware of much that went on anywhere other than her phone screen—protested and groaned at the request. "Leah, shut up and do as they say for once," he said.

"You don't tell *me* what to do. You're not my parent," Leah responded.

"Both of you, just go and wait in the lounge please," said Elaine.

"All right. What's the big deal?" said Leah. There was no answer.

Jake got up to take his plate into the kitchen. "Leave it, Jake," said Elaine. "I'll do it after."

"After what?" said Leah. Still no answer. "Jesus! Why doesn't anyone speak in this house?" She stormed into the lounge with her phone. Jake followed her. Slowly. Elaine looked at Hugh. He had his head tipped back, finishing a can of lager—he'd given up on trying not to have one at the table. Elaine tutted.

The ghosts, who had been listening from the sidelines, looked at each other in growing panic. They, too, knew what this signified. Penny frantically gestured to Sam to go upstairs and gather the remaining ghosts who weren't present. The rest of them followed the family into the lounge. The pastor, in his usual spot on the sofa, was surprised to see everyone traipsing in after dinner; he had to get out of the way quickly before he was sat on. As the family settled themselves, all pretty much as far apart as they could there were bumps and bangs from upstairs. Everyone looked up. They were all still a bit jumpy after the break-in. "Has someone got a window open?" said

Elaine. "No wonder it's so bloody cold in here." There were shrugs and shakes of the head.

"Shall I go and check?" said Hugh.

"No, leave it. Probably just the wind. Sit down," said Elaine.

Upstairs, Sam was charging about, trying to rouse the colonel and Calypso. "*They're having the conversation! They're having the conversation!*"

"What, *now?*" said the colonel, sitting up, bleary-eyed.

"Yes, now! In the lounge. Hurry!"

"I was dreading this day arriving, and here it is. We've failed. All of us have failed!" said the colonel. Sam left the room in search of Calypso. He found her in one of the spare rooms, her usual one. It was quiet in there. She rarely got disturbed.

"Calypso, wake up! They're having the conversation downstairs!"

"What conversation? Why're you waking me up when it's not dark, boy?" She peered at Sam from underneath the eye mask she wore whilst asleep.

"*The* conversation. They're telling Leah and Jake they're splitting up. We think, anyway."

"Good Lord, no," she said. "Well, you'd better be right, waking me up at this hour, young Sam. Go on with you, I'll be down in a minute. I need to put my face on. Wandering about in the light like this… I look like a ghost!"

"Hurry up then!" Sam joined the colonel on the landing, who was still buttoning up his waistcoat. They negotiated the stairs as quickly, but quietly, as they could together. As they entered the lounge, the rest of the ghosts looked up. They looked grave. Everyone looked grave.

Hugh was speaking. "Your mother and I..." He faltered. So many times he'd been over this in his head. So many times he'd practised wording it, but he never got that far because it always made him want to cry. "Your mother and I—"

"Leah, will you put your phone down please, your father is talking," said Elaine.

Leah groaned, rolled her eyes and relinquished her phone, stuffing it between her legs. But the interruption had broken Hugh's train of thought. God, this was hard. He needed another drink. He tried to speak again, but his lip quivered. His eyes welled up and he choked back a sob. The sob caught Leah's attention. Was Dad crying? Dad never cries.

Hugh heard Elaine sigh impatiently. "I'm afraid, children," she said, "what your father's trying to say is—and there's no easy way of saying this—that me and your dad are splitting up. We're putting the house on the market." Hugh shot her a look, thinking, *Jesus, when did you get so cold?* He looked back at his children, to see their reaction. He'd never seen Jake look so serious. Stony-faced, staring. Eyes glazed, weighing up the permutations. Leah looked incredulous as if she couldn't believe what she was hearing. Elaine continued. "We've tried, kids, we've really tried. But it's the best thing for all of us. None of us are happy like this. You don't want to hear us rowing all the time. It's a mutual decision..."

"*Mutual decision?*" said Leah, standing up. "Since when were *we* consulted on this? You're so bloody selfish, both of you! Just like we weren't consulted on moving out here, away from all my friends. And now we've got to move again? What was the point? I'm not moving schools if that's what you think! And no wonder you're both so miserable. All Dad does is drink, and all you bloody do is sleep! I hate you. Both of you!" And with that, she marched out of the room in tears, clutching her phone.

"Leah! Come back!" said Hugh, finding his voice. Elaine broke down then, sobbing. Hugh's first instinct was to go to her, to comfort her. But the invisible wall between them, the barrier, stopped him. They didn't do things like that anymore. He turned to his son instead. Jake's face was a confused picture of pain. He was trying not to cry, trying to be the man. Hugh went to him, sat down beside him. He put his hand on Jake's shoulder. Jake flinched, hurt and hard done to, not used to physical contact from his dad. Hugh squeezed his shoulder, tried to pull Jake towards him. He resisted. "Come on, it's all right," said Hugh. Jake finally caved in. His shoulders shook and he leant into his dad, breaking down in tears. Hugh held him, pulled him close, and Jake's baseball cap fell off. He stroked his son's soft rarely seen hair with a large hand, comforting him. Elaine watched them, feeling excluded, adrift—somehow detached yet guilty at the same time: as if she was the perpetrator of all this misery.

There was barely a dry eye in the house. Calypso, who had slipped in, was already in tears at the poignant scene that greeted her. Leah had run straight through her on the stairs. Penny and the twins were crying silently. So were the pastor and Sam. Cordingley was sniffling and wiping his glasses on his handkerchief. He wanted to blow his nose. Even the colonel was struggling to keep a stiff upper lip. He kept blinking as if he had something in his eye.

That night, Leah shunned both her parents' knocks on her door, their entreaties for understanding. It was too soon, too raw. *Just go away!* she said. This one was going to take a while, a while for her young brain to come to terms with, to see how it sat with her. At present, she couldn't see any further than how it affected her. This wasn't one that you posted on Facebook, like any other semi-significant event in her life. It was the opposite. It was embarrassing, mortifying: another thing to keep secret from her so-called friends. None of *their* parents were splitting up. They were all cosy, smug, happy families—or appeared to be; that or their parents were well down the line in second marriages or partnerships; got it over and done with whilst the kids were still young. How could her parents do this to her now? At this juncture in her life?

It made Leah want to hurt herself again. She searched for her badge, but it had gone missing. She pulled her pencil case out of her rucksack. Her compass was missing, too. "Shit!" She wanted someone to talk to, to take the pain away. There was only one person that she could confide in, to turn to for sympathy, to get it all out of her system to; one person who didn't go to school with her that wouldn't gossip about her and spread rumours behind her back. And that person was Ryan. As a result of his rejection, she had perversely placed him on a pedestal. He was seemingly the only answer, a light in the darkness. Sod it, she was going to swallow her pride and message him.

Throughout that evening, Leah sent various messages to Ryan. To her relief, they all went through. At least he hadn't blocked her. The messages started off casual, conversational, but became increasingly desperate in tone, as they remained unanswered.

6:45 p.m.: '*Hey, why aren't we friends anymore?*'

7:25 p.m.: '*Was it something I said?*'

7:51 p.m.: '*I miss u. x*'

8:25 p.m.: '*My parents are splitting up*'

103

9:01 p.m.: '*My house got broken into*'

At some point, she heard noises out in the corridor, from the room opposite. Banging about and drawers opening and closing. Then there was a knock on the door. Her dad popped his head in. "We're going to bed now. Are you OK?" Leah nodded. She didn't look OK. "You sure? Well, night then." He went to close the door.

"Dad?"

"Yes."

"What were you doing in that spare room?"

"Oh, I'm sleeping in there tonight. And probably from now on. It's for the best." He looked a little ashamed.

Hugh moving into a spare room made it more real for Leah, somehow. More definite. *So it was really happening then, this wasn't just another row*, she thought. It made her feel sorry for her dad.

9:35 p.m.: '*I want to hurt myself*'

The ghosts had watched Leah typing away in increasing horror and frustration, Penny with thin, taut lips, barely able to suppress her anger at the girl's stupidity. She wanted to slap her. The girl was poking the beast, inviting it back into her life, into this house. She could still remember how that *thing* had sniffed Leah's clothes; the delirious look on her face afterwards, as if she'd taken a hit of a drug. Sam looked mournful, worried. Cordingley was chomping at the bit to get involved; the minute Leah fell asleep, those unanswered messages were getting deleted.

****

From the squalor of her front room, sitting on her stinky, brown couch, Miss Collins had watched the messages come through. And with each notification, she was getting more and more twitchy. The temptation to reply was getting harder to resist. She should have blocked the damn girl; now she would know if the messages had been looked at or not.

After the incident at the house, Miss Collins had tried to move on, to pursue other avenues, to cast her net back out. But, truth be told, there was nothing else out there. It was a barren period. The fish weren't biting. And the ones she had made contact with were either too savvy or plain uninterested—dead ends. Also, now that the dust had settled and she'd had time to reflect on that night, it seemed unreal, something that couldn't have happened: something to laugh about in the cold light of day.

Now the girl was shaking the tree again, a fly caught in the web: a big, fat, juicy one that had been saved for a special occasion. And she wasn't just wriggling, causing the web to vibrate; she was practically twanging the line. Like a string on a harp. Over and over again. The prey taunting the predator, saying, 'Come and get me... I want to be caught.' She could sense the girl's desperation, her isolation, her neediness and vulnerability; her messages screamed for attention.

Oddly, it was the one about the break-in that finally swayed it for Miss Collins. She had left in such a rush that night. What had she left behind? What did the girl know? Wasn't it better to keep her onside? What if the police trawled through Leah's Facebook activity, her friends? Surely, she was the only member of the family young enough and stupid enough to have advertised that they were going away. Wouldn't the fact that she'd suddenly been unfriended without warning, at around the same time of the break-in, by a mystery boy that she'd never met, look odd?

It was ten o'clock. Leah was drifting off to sleep in her clothes, still clutching her tablet. The ghosts were circling, waiting, wondering how they were going to extract the gadget from her grasp. Suddenly, the device vibrated, making them all jump. Leah's eyes shot open in the dark. She grappled with her tablet to unlock it, the bright display screen hurting her eyes. '*New message from Ryan Daniels*'. Her heart jolted. She clicked on the notification. Ryan's little round profile picture came up. And a message: '*Hey. Sorry about your parents. That sucks.*' It was accompanied by a sad face emoji.

Like the tablet itself, Leah's face lit up in the dark. She emitted a half-laugh, half-sob. Then, biting her lip, she began typing frantically, pausing to wipe away a tear. '*Does this mean we're friends again?*' Send. She waited, gnawing at a nail. The device vibrated twice in quick succession. Two notifications—a new friend request from Ryan and another message. She laughed. And suddenly all the pain melted away.

Pressing accept, she checked out the message: '*Sorry for unfriending you. My mates said I was wasting my time, that u were stringing me along and would never meet me. They said u'd always be just a Facebook buddy. I shouldn't have listened to them*'.

God, no! *Poor thing*, she thought and began typing again: '*No. I wanted to meet u. I was going to tell u when I got back from holiday. I swear. x*'.

They messaged late into the night, picking up where they'd left off. About school, about music… But also about families and break-ups. Ryan's parents had split up, too, apparently, so he knew how it felt. He said it gets easier. This is what she had missed. This is what she needed; someone that understood her. Someone that cared. *'Listen to "Lego House", it reminds me of you,'* he said. She did. Leah fell in love that night. She wanted to meet Ryan, face to face, to hear his voice—not just to read his typed messages. They arranged to meet that coming Saturday morning at the bandstand in Oakham Park at eleven o'clock. The ghosts were beside themselves.

Chapter Eleven

In the days following the conversation, Leah and Jake noticed a marked change in their parents' behaviour. The children were the recipients of unwanted physical attention, syrupy-sweet affection. Offers of guilt money, concert tickets and computer games. It was too much, obsessive as if their parents were trying to outdo each other, to curry favour; channelling the love they couldn't show for each other into their children.

In regards to themselves, Hugh and Elaine communicated more. There were fewer silences. But the tone they had adopted with each other was of a more formal nature: business-like. Phone calls were made. Estate agents came to value the house. A 'For Sale' sign was put up at the bottom of the lane. It was a reminder of the impending break-up for the children every day as they left for school.

The ghosts had seen it all before. The house being sold. And they did their best to make nuisances of themselves whenever there was a viewing. Creating smells, messing up tidied rooms, making taps drip. They even tried but failed, to push over the 'For Sale' sign. It was a bit like the old days. They had played havoc with the previous family, as they hadn't liked them: the perpetrators of 'The Time of Great Unrest'. Clocks had been constantly changed, the thermostat was always being messed with, clothes and car keys had been hidden, the Sellotape, the scissors, the TV remote…

The ghosts' main concern at present, however, was how to stop this potentially devastating meeting between Leah and 'the beast' taking place. A couple of messages from Ryan had been successfully intercepted and deleted. But this had done little but cause temporary confusion. Meanwhile, the juggernaut rolled on. The colonel and Cordingley had devised a two-pronged attack for the big day, but the plan couldn't be put into action until the last minute.

Come the dreaded Saturday morning, Leah informed her parents that she was going ice-skating later with her friend, Abby. They were catching the bus into Leicester. Leah asked if someone would be able to give her a lift to the bus stop in town. Hugh was more than happy to oblige. It was something to do, a distraction. This suited Elaine; she had the weekly shop to do. The second Leah left her bedroom to have a shower, taking her phone with her: the ghosts sprang into action. They became regimental, soldier-like. "Right, men. Initiate phase one. Sam, lookout. Go!" said the colonel. Sam dashed out onto the landing. "Cordingley, tablet. Go!" Cordingley saluted and grabbed Leah's tablet from the bed. He had been practising this for days; it was his moment, his time to shine. The ghosts gathered around, crowding him. He fumbled with the device, almost dropping it.

"Quick, quick!" urged the twins as he dithered.

"Quiet! I need to concentrate. You're putting me under pressure! Right, I'm in."

"Hurry up! Send the message!" said Absinthe.

"I can't. There are adjustments to be made first! Accounts… settings… notifications—push, text, e-mail, mobile…" Click. Click. "I think that's it, all notifications are turned off."

"Now send the message!" said Juniper.

"Wait! Friends… messages… Ryan… Here we go." Cordingley began typing. '*Dear Ryan, Unfortunately, I shall be a little late to—*"

"Leah doesn't speak like that on these gadgets!" said Penny. "The beast will smell a rat. Here, let me do it." She tried to take the tablet.

"No. You've no experience of these things. We'll be here all day. This is my department!" protested Cordingley.

They wrestled over the tablet until the colonel hissed, "Pack it in. Both of you. Penny, let go. Leave the man to it!"

"Well, use some of those face things then," said Penny. "And type faster. Use your thumbs like Leah does! And pretend you're illiterate!"

"Sound American," chirped in Absinthe. "Start with 'hey'."

Cordingley gave them both a despairing look, then began typing again, prodding with his finger. '*Hey Ryan. Going to be—*'

"Not 'going', 'gonna'," said Penny.

'*Gonna be a bit late. Can't get a*'—delete 'a'—'*can't get lift till 11:30.*'

"Which face thing?" he asked.

"That one, with the exasperated expression. Like your face, Cordingley," Juniper mocked. "And put a kiss."

He did as she said. "Right, send."

"What if she doesn't reply, or doesn't get the message?" said Absinthe.

"We'll just have to pray," said the pastor.

Minutes passed. The ghosts waited nervously.

Sam burst in. "She's turned the shower off!"

"Damn," said the colonel. "Sam, get back out there. Keep your ears and eyes open."

"Come on," said Cordingley, tapping his foot.

"Damn, damn," said the colonel.

"I don't think you've thought this through, Cordingley. How can you delete a reply if—" The tablet vibrated, interrupting Penny. Cordingley looked at her smugly.

"What does it say? What does it say?" said Absinthe, jumping up and down.

"Wait... it says: '*Kk. C u then*'. What the hell does that mean?"

"Bloody kids and their damn codes. It's worse than the war!" said the colonel.

"No, wait. 'C u then' is 'see you then'," said Juniper.

"Well, what about 'kk'?" said Penny.

"If I had more time I'd be able to work it out," said Cordingley. "But at least the message was received. It worked."

"We haven't *got* time. Just delete the messages. Quickly!" said Penny.

Sam burst in again. "She's coming!" They heard the bathroom door out on the landing opening.

"Are they deleted?" said Absinthe.

"Yes!"

"Close it down, man. Close it down!" urged the colonel.

Cordingley pressed a few buttons and threw the device back onto the bed. Leah walked in with a towel wrapped around her body and one around her head. She smelt of the shower, and her arms and shoulders were goose-pimpled from the cold. Sam sniffed the air she left in her wake as she breezed by. Leah noticed her tablet lit up and walked over to it. She leant forward and swiped the screen. It was unlocked. That was funny. She checked the Facebook messenger icon. Nothing. She checked Instagram and Snapchat. Nothing. No new messages. Weird. She noticed the time on the screen and stood back up quickly; it was getting on. As she went to unwind the towel from her head, Penny made a signal for everybody to clear out. The ghosts filed out, but Sam lingered. Penny dragged him out by his ear.

Half an hour later, the ghosts watched from Leah's bedroom window as she got in the car. They were terrified for her, desperate. Sam felt like crying. But there was no time for sentiment. As soon as the car started up, the colonel barked, "Cordingley, initiate phase two! Go!"

Cordingley already had the tablet in his hands. He fired it up and negotiated his way straight to Mr Berridge's e-mail account. He'd also been practising this—how to send an e-mail. Subject: *URGENT!* Message: *HELP. A POTENTIAL KIDNAP IS TAKING PLACE AT OAKHAM PARK BANDSTAND AT 11:30 A.M. TODAY. THIS IS NOT A HOAX. IT INVOLVES A 13-YEAR-OLD GIRL AND A MIDDLE-AGED WOMAN POSING AS A YOUNG BOY. I REPEAT THIS IS NOT A HOAX. THE GIRL'S LIFE IS AT A RISK. THERE IS NO TIME TO WASTE! ANON.* Enter recipient: easterncounties.npa@rutlandpolice.co.uk. Send.

"Is it done?" said the colonel.

"It's done."

"Right, delete it!"

"I am doing!" Cordingley deleted the message. He made sure Gmail notifications were turned on, just in case, then placed the tablet back on the bed. A silence descended. Their job was done. They could do no more. Only fate could decide what happened to poor Leah now.

"I would like us all to join hands," said the pastor. "Let us pray for Leah's safe return."

****

Leah and Hugh were on the short car journey into town. Hugh tried to make conversation, asking Leah if she was OK. But Leah was unresponsive; she had other things on her mind. She felt nervous, really nervous. She pretended to be engrossed in her phone, even though she had no Wi-Fi. Hugh watched his daughter in the rear-view mirror. She was wearing makeup, a bit more than usual when she met her friends. *When did she get so grown-up?* It made him want to cry. *When did I lose you?* he thought. Same with Jake—lost him to the computer games. Hugh felt as if he'd failed; they both had—he *and* Elaine; they hadn't tried hard enough. "You're not meeting any boys at the ice-skating rink, I hope?" he joked. Leah just looked at him. "Do you want me to drop you at Abby's house?"

"No, I'm meeting her at the bus stop."

"Well, you've got a few minutes yet. Do you want me to swing by and pick her up?"

"No, the bus stop's fine."

"OK… you're not ashamed of your old man, are you?" Another joke that fell on deaf ears. "Do you need some pocket money?" he tried.

"No, Mum gave me some." *Typical*, he thought, *got there before me.*

Hugh dropped Leah at the bus stop. There was a gaggle of older boys larking about, smoking. It made Hugh feel uncomfortable. "You're sure you don't want me to wait?" Leah was already out of the car. She closed the door. Hugh wound down his window. "Leah?" *What now?* She groaned. The boys were watching, and she blushed. *Please don't ask for a kiss; please don't ask for a kiss.* Her dad pulled a crumpled-up tenner out of his pocket. He pressed it into her hand, saying, "Enjoy yourself. And don't talk to any strange men!" Leah rolled her eyes in response. He kept his eye on her in the mirror as he drove away. She was fiddling with her phone.

Leah had got 3G. She briefly checked her messages. There weren't any. *This is it then*, she thought. Her stomach was in knots as she set off for the park. "*Where you going, gorgeous?*" one of the boys called after her. They all laughed. Leah ignored them and pulled some chewing gum out of her pocket. The menthol gum made her sneeze; it always did. "Shit!" *Bad idea*, she thought. She checked her nose in her phone camera, then checked the rest of her image. She considered sending a Snapchat: '*Going to meet Ryan. Wish me luck!*' But she didn't. She hadn't told anyone that she was meeting him, just in case he didn't show up. Leah sped up; she was going to be a few minutes late. Oh well, at least she wouldn't look too keen.

She entered the park through the east gate. It was a large, bowl-shaped park, surrounded by trees and grass banks, with a circular path to its perimeter. There were humps and hollows that kids raced BMXs over, a skateboard park and ramp; and your usual playground equipment: zip-wires, large swing baskets and so forth. The park was fairly deserted. It was cool for the time of year, breezy. There was one couple and a few single mums, all with toddlers, in the enclosed younger playpen, and a few skaters on the ramp, mainly youngsters, probably making the most of it before the older kids turned up. The sound of their boards cracked and echoed across the park.

The bandstand was in the middle of the lawned area of the park, a fair distance from anything else. It looked dark and shadowy inside it from afar but appeared to be empty. Leah couldn't be sure, though. Her heart sped up as she began walking down one of the artery paths towards it. She kept looking at her phone as she approached, trying to appear casual, in case she was being watched. 3G was fading, all but gone. Unable to resist it any longer, she looked up, expecting a boy to emerge from the shadows of the bandstand, leaning on the railings, watching out for her. Her knight in shining armour. Would he have a quiff as she'd imagined, or would he be wearing his cap?

To her disappointment, the bandstand was empty. She climbed the rusty steps to it, running her hands over the chipped paint of the railings. The wind had got up, and an empty plastic bottle was trapped, circling the interior, going around and around. Did she sit down, or lean on the railings to wait, affecting a grown-up pose like Juliet or Rapunzel, hair blowing in the breeze? She scanned the perimeter of the park. No sign of Ryan yet, just a lone woman in the distance in jogging gear; at least she thought it was a woman. Leah checked her phone again. Still no 3G, still no messages. She sat down to wait.

Meanwhile, back at the house, an unexpected e-mail reply had come through on Leah's tablet: *Sir/Madam. Can we please have your name, telephone number and home address?*

"What do we do?" said Penny.

"Well, give it to them, of course," said the colonel.

"What are they messing about at? Why aren't they helping Leah?" said Absinthe.

"I'm sure they are. They don't just have one police officer, you know," said Cordingley.

"Give them the address and phone number—quickly—just in case!" said Penny. Cordingley typed a reply and pressed send.

"Who's at home?" asked the colonel.

"Jake and Elaine, I think," said Penny.

"Elaine went out shopping," said Sam.

"Great. What if they ring up, needing more details or something?" said Penny.

"If they ring up, then they'll know that we sent the message," said Juniper.

"They'll know anyway, these things can be traced like phones," said Cordingley.

"Who cares if they know? Leah's safety is all that matters," said the pastor.

"Delete the messages anyway," said the colonel.

Just then, the phone rang out from the master bedroom and downstairs, startling them. It sent some of the ghosts into a panic. They ran out onto the landing and began pacing aimlessly back and forth. The phone carried on going, shrill, persistent—five, six, seven rings—but nobody answered it.

"Why isn't Jake answering the phone? How can he not hear it?" said Penny.

"He's probably got his headphones on," said Sam.

The phone rang off. "Damn it," said the colonel.

A few moments later there was a cry from Cordingley. It was the police station, e-mailing again: *Sir/Madam. Are you currently at the home address you gave us?* Cordingley looked to the colonel for instructions.

"Yes. Type 'yes', man!" Cordingley did as he was told.

Another e-mail came through. It said simply: *Answer the phone.*

The phone started ringing again. The noise was irritating, fractious. "Why won't the boy answer that damn phone!" said the colonel. Absinthe had an idea, and she ran to Jake's room. Without even pausing, she turned the handle on his door and pushed it open. Juniper, who had followed her sister, gasped as the door swung inwards. The rest of the ghosts held their hands over their mouths and waited with bated breath. They heard Jake's chair squeak as he got up.

A cricket bat, then a baseball-capped head, complete with headphones, slowly appeared, both sticking out of the doorway at an angle. Then Jake's wide eyes appeared, oscillating from side to side in his head. It would have been comical under other circumstances. He removed his headphones, a worried look on his face. He registered the phone ringing but didn't go to answer it. "Mum?" he called. Jake listened for a response, for noises in the house, his eyes still darting back and forth. It was hard to hear anything over the phone. He tiptoed across the landing, bat in hand, to his parents' room—well, just his mum's room these days. Pushing the door back hard, he burst in. The room was empty: no one behind the door. He went to answer the phone; it was driving him mad. "Hello." The ghosts crept in to listen.

At this point, there was the sound of keys rattling in the front door, and Elaine walked in, laden down with shopping bags. "Jake!" she called up the stairs. "Can you help me with the shopping please?" She waited for a reply, but all she heard instead was Jake's muffled voice talking to someone. *Must be on his headset*, she thought. "*Jake!*" she hollered again, then went back outside to get more shopping. By the time she'd returned, Jake was at the bottom of the stairs. "Oh, there you are! I've—"

"Mum, the police are on the phone," Jake cut in, breathlessly.

"What?"

"The police are on the phone, something about an e-mail sent from this address. Something about a kidnap."

"Jake, if this is a wind-up I haven't got time for it." She studied his face. It was pale, serious.

"Mum, I'm deadly serious. They're on the phone, now. Hurry!"

Elaine dropped the shopping bags and ran into the lounge. She picked up the phone. Jake ran upstairs to the other phone, listened for a moment, then put it back down. He raced back downstairs to the lounge. His mum was talking. "No, I can assure you I haven't. I've been shopping. I've only just walked through the door." She listened for a moment, her face grave. "Hold on, I'll ask him." She put the phone to her chest. "Jake, answer me truthfully. Have you sent a prank e-mail to the police? You won't get in trouble: just tell me the truth. Leah could be in danger. Answer me now!" *Maybe he was playing up in reaction to them splitting up. Don't they say this happens?*

"No, Mum. I swear I haven't. Why would I?" He looked earnest. She believed him. He wasn't that kind of boy. Panic set in.

"Hello! He says he hasn't. I believe him…" Her voice was beginning to wobble. "She's ice-skating with her friend. My husband dropped them in town at the bus stop… About eleven o'clock." Jake watched his mum's face drain of colour; her eyes grow wide in horror as she listened. "Oh my god. I will. I'll call her. But go to the park! Please. Now. I beg you!" Her voice was getting hysterical.

"Mum, what's going on?" said Jake.

"I will. Goodbye." Elaine slammed the phone down. "Shit! Where's my mobile!" She patted her pockets.

"Mum! What's going on?" The hysteria was contagious.

"It's Leah, she might be in trouble. Oakham police station received an anonymous tip-off about a middle-aged woman meeting a girl at the park. Shit! Where's my bloody phone?"

"It's probably in your bag."

Elaine ran out to the hallway where her handbag was hanging on the bannister post. Jake followed her out.

"A middle-aged woman?" said Jake. "Are they sure it's not one of her friends messing about?"

Elaine pulled out her phone. "Shit, shit, shit. Where's her number? Messages… Call."

"She's probably just ice-skating."

"Shut up, Jake. I can't hear! Sorry. It's ringing. Please pick up, Leah. Please pick up."

Just then, there was the sound of a car pulling up on the drive. Jake ran to the door. "It's Dad. He's back."

"Is he on his own?"

"Yes."

****

Leah's phone lit up and began vibrating. It was her mum. *Flippin' hell, what does she want? And where was Ryan?* It was getting on for quarter past now. Leah considered ignoring the call but then decided against it. She might need a lift home at this rate. *But then how did she explain that one? She should be on the bus into town by now. Missed the bus?* She didn't want to go back home, though. Better to go to Abby's for a bit instead.

As Leah put the phone to her ear, saying, "Hi, Mum," a figure walked past the bandstand. Leah turned to look, thinking, *if that's Ryan, and I'm on the phone to my bloody mum...* It wasn't. It was the woman she had seen in the distance. Her hands were stuffed into her grey hoody pockets. She turned her head briefly towards the bandstand, stared right at Leah, then carried on walking.

"Leah? Thank God! Where are you? The signal's bad," said Elaine.

"I'm on the bus into town, where do you think?"

"I can't hear the bus. Is Abby with you?"

"Yes, why?"

"Leah, don't lie to me. Is Abby with you?"

"Yes!"

"Put her on then."

"Mum, you're being ridiculous."

"No, Leah. I'm being deadly serious. Listen to me. Don't be alarmed, you're not in trouble, but the police have called here—and I know it sounds daft—but it was something about a woman posing as a boy, something about you meeting him in the park in town. You're not in the park, are you?"

120

Leah didn't answer.

"Leah! Tell me you're not in the park!"

"Mum, you're scaring me!"

"Leah. Tell me you're not in the park. You're not in the bandstand, are you?"

Leah's stomach sank.

"Oh, Mum," she whimpered.

"Leah, you stupid girl!" Leah let out a sob. "I'm sorry, I'm sorry. I didn't mean that. The main thing is that you're safe. Just get up and walk away. Keep your phone on. Keep talking to me, and walk out of the park, towards the shops."

Leah couldn't get out of there quick enough. She clanged down the steps of the bandstand on legs that didn't seem to want to support her. Miss Collins registered the noise. She had been standing with her back against the rear of the bandstand, feeling the reverberations of Leah's voice through the thin metal, listening to her conversation. Wait, wait, she told herself, clenching and unclenching the handle of the knife in her hoody pocket. Keep your distance, there's still a chance yet. Keep cool, wait till we're in the trees at the edge of the park.

Miss Collins counted to ten—slowly—it was agony. Then she peered around the edge of the bandstand. Leah was 20 to 30 yards away, further than expected, already a third of the way down the path to the edge of the park. Miss Collins set off after her at a brisk pace, almost a jog. Leah was still on her phone, still talking, looking around her, looking everywhere but behind her. Miss Collins was gaining on her, bit by bit. That's it, keep looking ahead, little girl, keep looking ahead.

At that moment, Leah turned around for the first time. She was more than halfway down the path. Briefly, she registered the woman in the grey hoody and jogging bottoms behind her then turned back around. Miss Collins sped up, jogging now. Leah turned back around to take another look. The woman was getting closer, her eyes honed in on her, her face grim, determined, menacing. Leah let out a scream as it dawned on her who she was. "Mum! She's here. She's following me!" She broke into a run. Miss Collins ran too. People in the toddler's enclosure looked over at the commotion.

"*Leah!*" cried Elaine. But Leah didn't answer. She was sprinting now, clutching her phone. Through the trees up ahead, she could see the gate to the street and traffic going past. Elaine was beside herself. All she could hear was the pounding of feet and her daughter whimpering. Every parent's worst nightmare. "*Leah!*"

Leah reached the trees, hurtling down the path between them, eyes focused on the gate ahead, not daring to look behind her. Surely she had put some distance between her and the woman—she had looked out of shape. Leah reached the gate, crying, breathless, scrabbling at the goddamn bar on it that was too stiff to open. Her phone was hampering her. It slipped out of her grasp, tumbling to the floor. Elaine was in hysterics now, screaming down the phone. Leah went to pick it up, frantically looking behind her, unable to help herself. She expected a pudgy hand on her shoulder, that malevolent twisted red face behind her. It wasn't. The woman was nowhere to be seen. She picked up her phone. The screen was cracked. "Shit!"

She managed to open the gate, the phone still in hand, her dad's voice coming out of it now as well: "*Leah! Talk to us!*"

And then she was out. Blessed pavement. Cars. People. She was still looking behind her, speaking into her phone,

"Mum, I'm okay—" when she banged into someone. A surprised female voice cried out. Leah screamed again and began to pummel the body of the person with her fists. Elaine joined in, screaming down the phone.

"It's okay, I'm a police officer. You're safe." The lady held Leah's wrists.

Leah looked up; a kind, motherly face under a black cap, a blonde ponytail spilling over a black vest. Leah broke down in relief, wanting her own mum.

"Where is she?" the officer said, letting go.

"In there," Leah pointed. "In the park." Her voice was shaky.

A male police officer appeared.

"She's in the park," the female officer said.

"Stay here," the male officer said. He ran off into the park, speaking into his police radio.

The lady put a hand on Leah's shoulder. "It's OK, you're safe now. We'll get her."

Leah cradled her phone to her ear. She could hear her mum and dad crying. "Mum, Dad. It's OK. I'm safe. I'm with the police."

"Oh, thank you, God, thank you, God," said Elaine.

"Mum, I'm sorry," Leah sobbed, "about everything. Dad too. Tell him."

"I'm here, baby, I'm listening," Hugh cut in, his voice wobbling.

"About the way I've been acting lately. I've been so stupid…"

"No. Shush now, baby. You're safe now, that's all that matters," said Elaine.

Miss Collins was rugby-tackled to the ground by an over-enthusiastic police officer, waiting on the other side of the park. Her grey hood flew back to reveal her shaved and tattooed head. In her possession were a flick knife and a bandana—the type used for blindfolding and gagging purposes.

In her foul-smelling home, no less than three laptops were found, several fake IDs, various wigs and disguises, numerous weapons—including nunchucks, knives and rope—and breaking-in paraphernalia, such as bolt cutters, balaclavas and crowbars.

On her laptops, dozens of fake online profiles were found, all with trails and footprints—some defunct, some ongoing—providing evidence of child grooming (all girls), and attempted child-kidnap. Also, dozens of galleries of young girls were found—Leah being the latest favourite. During the search, the woman's past criminal and medical history came out, along with her real identity—a Miss Janet Cragg. Already known to the police and considered a menace. In particular, to young girls. She was looking at serious jail time.

Hugh and Elaine were horrified that this had happened to one of their own, right under their very noses—that they had taken their eyes off the ball that badly. They blamed themselves. The detective in charge said that they shouldn't. It could have been any young girl in the area. "Deviants like Cragg cast their net far and wide," he said. "They are chancers, widely referred to these days as 'catfish' and Cragg was a persistent, compulsive catfish. They do their homework, do their research, ask the right questions, and home in on the vulnerable, the lonely—those desperate for attention and affection." Elaine had sobbed at this. "They are very clever at seeking out children from single-parent families, or that have fragmented unstable home lives. Sometimes, it's as if the child almost *wants* to be caught—I don't mean literally; that would be ridiculous—but bonding with a stranger online can provide a form of escape, or serve as an act of rebellion in reaction to something. Tell me, I don't mean to pry—has there been some instability lately, a disagreement or shock in the family? I noticed the 'For Sale' sign…"

The Berridges looked at each other guiltily. "Only the house going on the market, really," said Hugh.

The detective appeared to consider this as he took a welcome sip of coffee. His hands were cold. He returned his cup to the coffee table and picked up some leaflets he had brought with him. "Going forward, here's some useful information on keeping children safe online." He passed the leaflets to Elaine.

"Oh, trust me. This won't be happening again!" she said dismissively.

"Take a look anyway. There's some good stuff, things that might not occur to a child—or to an adult for that matter. Not posting your whereabouts on Facebook for example— 'checking in' as they call it—or not keeping your Facebook GPS on: it's practically advertising your location to these people. And trust me, they use this stuff. I hear you had a break-in recently, here at the house, whilst you were away. Yet nothing was taken. Did any of you mention the fact that you were going away on social media? Post your whereabouts?"

Elaine looked guilty again. "Maybe…" she said.

"Because we're pretty certain that the break-in was by Cragg, and we intend to nail her for it as well. Again, it would be textbook catfish behaviour. I know this will sit uncomfortably with you both as parents, and I apologise for that, but Cragg *was* obsessed with your daughter." Elaine shuddered and leant into Hugh. Surprised, he put his arm around her for support. "She would have seen that you were all away, possibly posted by Leah, and would have been looking for information, or some sort of connection, to further her cause. Maybe even something of Leah's to take away with her."

"But why *didn't* she take anything, then?" said Hugh.

"Who knows? Maybe she got disturbed by someone, which leads me to my next point—we still haven't established who sent the tip-off e-mail. To this end, and to help establish if it *was* Cragg that broke in, we are going to have to take away all electronic devices from the household for analysis—laptops, tablets, phones, etc." The Berridges let out a groan of displeasure at this. "Don't worry, nobody is in trouble. We just need to identify the device that the e-mail was sent from—to rule out the possibility of Cragg having an accomplice. The e-mail was sent from your account wasn't it, Mr Berridge?"

"Yes, but I wasn't even here at the time."

"But you had your phone on you at the time, I take it?"

"Yes, but—"

"There lies my point."

"You're not suggesting—"

"We're not suggesting anything; you've all been through enough. It's just a matter of procedure when we receive a tip-off, whether it be for a fire alert, a bomb threat—or anything—we have to establish the source. It was just your son—Jack, is it?—that was here at home in the minutes leading up to the attempted kidnap?"

"Jake," said Elaine.

"Sorry, Jake. He was the one who answered the phone, wasn't he?"

"Yes," confirmed Elaine, "but I hope you're not suggesting that he was involved somehow either, a prank or something? Why would he do that? Why would any of us do that if our daughter was in real danger? It doesn't make sense!" Elaine broke down and leant into Hugh again. She felt protective of her son, of her whole family. By having their devices taken away, it somehow felt as if they were under suspicion themselves, connected to all this in some way. The detective was right. They had been through enough already. She just wanted him to piss off and leave; leave her family to work through what had happened together, alone.

"You're right, Mrs Berridge. It doesn't make sense. You see, someone could have hijacked Mr Berridge's account—a work colleague, for example. We need to make sure no one else was involved in this, eliminate all possibilities... We also need to analyse Leah's social media activity leading right up to the time of the attempted abduction."

"It's fine, Detective, take what you need. We need to get to the bottom of it," said Hugh.

"Thank you for your co-operation. And give those leaflets a read; they're worth it." The detective stopped to finish the last of his coffee then briskly rubbed his hands together. "These old buildings take a while to warm up in summer, don't they?" he said.

****

The ghosts had listened to the whole conversation. They retreated to the stable block to confer. "They're taking the gadgets. All of the gadgets!" said Cordingley.

"Good. Hopefully, they'll keep them," said Penny. "I blame the gadgets."

"Yes, we know you blame the gadgets," said Juniper.

"But they'll know! The police will know that we sent it!" said Cordingley.

"Calm down, man," said the colonel. "They won't know that *we* sent it. They'll know that *somebody* sent it. You're missing the bigger picture here. The main thing is that Leah is safe. The operation was a success. We did it. Between us, we did it. We kept Leah safe!"

"But what if Mr Berridge gets in trouble? Or Jake?" said Sam.

"They won't," said the colonel.

Chapter Twelve

The Berridge family were none-too-pleased about having their electronic devices taken away. It was an invasion of privacy for a start. What secrets would be unveiled? Jake had it the worst, bless him, what with being under suspicion; he had to have his fingerprints taken, too. He didn't even have his Xbox to seek solace in. This had left him somewhat stunned at first. It was as if he'd been detached from an iron lung or life support machine. He had to learn to breathe on his own again, to take part in the real world. *What do you do out there? What is the Sun? What is grass?*

For Elaine, it was the same with Facebook. *How could she not look at Facebook? It was an addiction.* And thank God. she'd never sent that message to her old boyfriend from school. As for Hugh, he had to go 'old school' and use the red button on the television set and the newspaper to keep up with the latest sports news. He had to stay at work longer, too, as he could no longer send e-mails from home. Funnily enough, it was Leah, the most persistent social media addict—her phone was practically an extension of her body—that was the least bothered by it all. The whole Cragg episode had shocked her, and well, it would. It had put her off the internet for a while. She'd read the leaflets the detective had left and was heeding some of their advice.

This enforced 'electronic cold turkey' had left most of the Berridges miserable at first, grumpy. But after a few days, it got easier. Slowly, they came out of their hidey-holes, were forced together as a family: just what the ghosts had wanted. They even watched TV together a bit.

The police never did get to the bottom of who sent the tip-off. But it was a strange one that had them baffled. Once they'd established the e-mail was sent from Leah's tablet, this ruled Mr Berridge out of the equation. Mrs Berridge too. At first, it looked for all the world like the ultimate cry for help, the girl putting herself in potential danger to get noticed, echoing the detective's words. But there was no evidence whatsoever to suggest that Leah thought Ryan was anyone other than who he said he was—an innocent, teenage boy. Besides, the timings were wrong. According to Mr Berridge's account of the day, Leah was already in the car with him at the time that the e-mail was sent. She didn't have her tablet on her and had nowhere to hide it. She certainly didn't have it on her when she bumped into the police.

Which led them to the boy, Jake. He was the only one that could have sent it. There were some worrying moments for a while, but again, ultimately, this solution didn't add up. There weren't any of his fingerprints on the device for a start, he didn't even know her password; something the whole family were adamant about. Why would he? It was like giving your teenage sibling access to your personal diary. Plus, he seemed like a good kid. His school records were exemplary. And why would he risk putting his sister in mortal danger? His beloved Xbox came to his rescue, too. Jake's online records showed that he was gaming at the time that the e-mail was sent, talking to his mates.

So, it remained a mystery. The police were satisfied that Cragg wasn't involved with anyone else—these people rarely were. Catfish were loners, selfish, unwilling to share their prizes. The main thing was that the girl was safe—hopefully, she'd learnt her lesson—and that Janet Cragg would be going away for a long time. They'd managed to pin the break-in on her, too. Prints taken from the house had matched hers.

****

To celebrate the news—and the safe return of their devices—the Berridges all went out for a meal at their favourite local Indian restaurant. But in keeping with a new regime that Elaine had proposed, all phones were kept out of sight (and use) during the meal. Without the distraction of them, the family actually had a decent conversation for once. Elaine got her molten curry at last, and she and Hugh reminisced and laughed over a couple of bottles of Indian beer. It felt like old times.

When they got back home, to her parents' surprise, Leah suggested that they watch a film together. "Your choice, Dad," she said. Jake mumbled that he'd got nothing better to do and that he'd make some popcorn.

"Let's have a vote then," said Hugh, thrilled. *Weird Science* came out on top.

Elaine and Hugh cracked open a bottle of wine, sitting on one sofa, whilst the children shared a bowl of popcorn, sitting on the other. Elaine spread a blanket over her and Hugh's legs, as she was cold. The children nudged each other and smiled.

The ghosts sat around, watching too, glowing with contentment. Their attention split between the family and the film. Sam was on the floor at Leah's feet. The twins were holding hands. The colonel and Penny were both looking smug. Cordingley was scratching his arms and tutting to himself at all the technological improbabilities in the film.

Elaine managed to stay awake throughout the whole thing, which was a first in a while. As the credits rolled at the end, she yawned, stretched and said, "Hugh, can you give the estate agents a ring tomorrow, tell them to come and take that sign down?" Hugh looked across at her, raised his eyebrows, and smiled.

"Listen, a minute," said Leah, interrupting their moment. "Can you hear that? Jake, turn the sound down." She smacked his leg.

Jake tutted but did as she said.

The Berridges held their breath and listened.

From somewhere in the living room was the distinct sound of a cat purring.

The End